L.M. Merrington was
holds a Bachelor of Arts in media and communications
and Chinese, and a PhD in international relations, and
has worked as a freelance journalist, editor, strategic
analyst and communications manager.

She lives in Canberra with her husband Tristan.
Greythorne is her first novel. Her website is
lmmerrington.com, and you can follow her on
Facebook at facebook.com/lmmerrington.

Greythorne

L.M. Merrington

PAC BOOKS

First published by Momentum in 2015
This edition published in 2017 by PAC Books
www.pacbooks.com.au

A CIP record for this book is available at the National Library of Australia

Greythorne

EPUB format: 9780648021544
Mobi format: 9780648021551
Print-on-demand format: 9780648021537

Cover design by Raewyn Brack
Edited by Kate O'Donnell
Proofread by Lauren Choplin

For Tristan

Chapter 1

"I'll take it from here, miss," the porter said, hefting my trunk onto his barrow with practiced ease. I smiled and gave him a coin, like Matron had told me to, watching with some apprehension as he wheeled the barrow deftly down the platform, dodging through the crowd. All my worldly possessions were in that trunk.

The railway station was, as all railway stations are, a place of noise, dust, smoke and heat. I was no stranger to train travel, for the Brookvale Girls Home, where I had spent my childhood, took all its girls on a day trip to the seaside every summer as a special treat, and I had always loved it – the sense of journeys beginning and ending, the possibilities. I knew this time it would be different, for I would not be returning to Brookvale, but even through the apprehension curling in my stomach I could not help but feel a thrill of excitement.

I stood on the platform for a moment – for I had arrived rather early – breathing in the sooty, metallic smell of the engine, my heart thrilling with excitement. Trunks and boxes crashed as they were loaded and unloaded from the train, breaking through the bustling chatter of the passengers searching for their carriages or engaging in emotional farewells with loved ones. I enjoyed watching the people most of all. Gathered near the first-class carriages were ladies wearing improbably tall hats and fine gowns of purple and blue and red, escorted by equally distinguished gentlemen. Farther down the platform, by the second-class carriages, were people of more my sort – farmers and their wives returning from a visit to town, and shop-girls or servants heading home to see their families – and in the middle of it all, me, a new would-be governess in a plain grey frock. No one even glanced my way, and why should they? I was utterly unremarkable.

"All aboard!" The guard's cry – unexpectedly loud for such a small man – cut through my reverie, and I scrambled into the train, stumbling on the step. I righted myself quickly, hoping no one had noticed, and made my way to a compartment, which, thankfully, was empty.

Settling into my seat, I glanced out the window at the frenetic last-minute preparations. Then the train blew its whistle and lurched forward. My old life now lay behind me – there could be no going back.

As the train began to pick up speed I reached into my scruffy old carpetbag and withdrew the note Matron had given me. It was hard to believe it had been only yesterday that she called me into her study and, with a few words, changed the course of my life.

"We have found you a situation," she had said. "We were contacted by a Professor Nathaniel Greythorne, of Greythorne Manor, —shire, who seeks a governess for his eight-year-old daughter, Sophie. I have been in correspondence with Professor Greythorne, and he seems a man of good breeding and good sense; he is a scientist. The child's mother has been dead these five years past, and he feels it high time she was exposed to a woman's influence, lest she grow up wild and uncultured." She had paused, then quoted from the letter: "*The place in which Greythorne Manor resides is a lonely, isolated spot, and thus the governess must not be of the temperament to pine for society or gaiety, for she will not find it here. She must be a sensible, practical girl, but not of a disposition so dour that mirth is a stranger to her.*

"I confess, Nell, on reading this I thought of you, for you are not averse to keeping your own company, and are a girl of good sense."

This was high praise indeed from Matron, and I had been unable to keep from blushing. I was also weak with relief, for although I had learned all the arts – academic, social, and domestic – that would prepare me for life as a governess to young ladies of good breeding, my lack of any sort of connections had made obtaining a situation difficult. One by one my peers had been sent out into the world, while I languished inside Brookvale's walls. Having just turned eighteen, I ought to have been cast out to fend for myself long ago, situation or no, but Matron was a kind-hearted woman beneath her gruff exterior, and I believe she was loath to give me over to a life of likely poverty. This news could not have come at a more opportune moment.

And so it had been decided that I was to be the new governess at Greythorne Manor, effective immediately. The preparations, it turned out, had already been made, and so I had barely had time to collect my belongings and my wits before setting out on the long journey north.

"You will take the train tomorrow to the village of Grimly," Matron had said. "You will need to change to the branch line, but it is not a difficult transition, and I am sure you are more than capable. But the journey is long and the train does not arrive until the early evening. You will be met at the station and will spend the night at the Grimly inn, before traveling on to Greythorne Manor in the morning. I believe the Professor will send someone to escort you. Whilst I am not convinced of the propriety of a young woman spending a night alone in an inn, it seems we have no choice. For reasons unclear to me, it is not possible to travel to Greythorne Manor after dark, though the Professor assures me it is merely a matter of logistics."

She had dismissed me then, condemning me to a night of teeming and anxious thoughts. Why could one not travel to the Manor after dark? What sort of man was the Professor? And, more importantly, what of the child, Sophie – a girl who had grown up all but motherless, and by her father's account was on the verge of becoming an uncouth wildling? I would know all soon enough, but at that moment my head was spinning.

As the train rattled along I read the Professor's letter again, but it yielded no further information. I sighed and tucked it back into my bag. There was nothing for it but to be patient.

I was staring out the window, lost in reverie, when I felt the train begin to slow, and soon we were pulling into a station on the outskirts of the city. There weren't many people on the platform, but as the locomotive blew its whistle the door to my compartment opened and a plump, matronly lady bustled in, juggling baskets and parcels. She was a rotund, cheerful sort, with apple-red cheeks and a ready smile. The train lumbered forward, catching her by surprise, and she stumbled; I half-rose and held out a hand to assist her.

"Eh now, thank you, love," she said. "You'd think it were my first time on a train." She laughed at herself, and I bit back a smile, suddenly shy around this stranger, but she seemed unfazed by my reticence.

"You don't mind if I sit by you?" she asked. I shook my head. "Grand. I'm Elsie – Elsie Drabble."

"Nell Featherstone."

"Pleased to meet you. Well, this is lovely. It's such a blessing to have someone to talk to on a long journey."

And talk she did. She was a type of person I rather liked, happy to carry on a conversation with very little input from me. She told me she was a farmer's wife from far to the north, returning home after spending a month with her daughter's family in the city.

"And right glad of it I am too," she said, "for I'm getting far too old for chasing after little ones, and my Katie has four and another one on the way. But it were a fair treat to see them all – the youngest hadn't yet been born when I was there last. But raising chickens is a fair sight easier than raising children, even though I've six of my own – all grown now, of course."

I nodded and smiled, though I found it hard to relate to her predicament. Of course, I'd helped look after the younger children at Brookvale, but could hardly be said to have raised them, and I'd certainly never kept chickens. And yet from tomorrow I would have almost full responsibility for the upbringing and education of a half-wild little girl. The thought excited and terrified me in equal measure.

"And where are you bound?" Mrs. Drabble asked. I glanced out the window. The train had left the periphery of the town behind it, and for some time we had been traveling through open countryside; the railway cut through a wide expanse of wild, rolling hills.

"Grimly," I said. "I have to change to the branch line to get there; it's a small town and not on the main way." I endeavored to sound as if I knew it well.

"Aye, I know Grimly," Mrs. Drabble said, beaming. "It's the closest town to our farm. Though it's more a village than a town, really, perched right up on the cliffs above the sea. Jack and me always catch the train from there if we're going to the city, not that we do very often. I can show you where to change trains. Visiting relatives, are you?"

"No … I'm engaged to be the new governess at Greythorne Manor."

Mrs. Drabble's countenance dropped; her cheerful, friendly eyes were suddenly hooded. "Greythorne Manor, you say? Are you sure?"

"Yes, of course."

"And do you know much of the place?"

"No, not at all – only that I've been engaged by Professor Greythorne to teach his daughter, Sophie … and that it's impossible to travel to the Manor after dark. Why is that so?"

"It's a windswept, isolated place, is Greythorne Manor," Mrs. Drabble said, not quite answering my question. "But if I were you, love, I wouldn't be going there at all, darkness or no. There's strange things afoot in that place, you mark my words. It hasn't been the same since the mistress died some five years back." And with that she snapped her mouth shut and would not be drawn further on the house or its occupants, no matter how carefully I probed. In the end I gave up and fell into a half-trance as the countryside swept by outside the window, until the locomotive began to slow and I knew we were reaching the terminus where I must change trains.

I had half-expected Mrs. Drabble to lose me in the crowd at the station, but to my surprise she seemed to have recovered from her malaise, and guided me companionably by the elbow to the little branch-line train.

This train was far smaller than the one from the city, with only a single carriage for passengers. Besides Mrs. Drabble and myself there were only three others, all of whom had the look of locals. I felt very far from home. But of course, whatever home I'd had was no longer there; the only way was onward.

The shadows were beginning to lengthen now, the last golden rays of the dying sun slanting in through the windows, for we were still traveling north. Mrs. Drabble pulled out a pair of knitting needles and a skein of wool; despite her brief helpfulness, she now seemed disinclined to talk. The other passengers were all engaged in their own pursuits, either reading or simply looking out the window, so I did the same. Too agitated to read – for an increasing nervous tension had come upon me with Mrs. Drabble's words, and especially now that my journey was so near its end – I once again stared out at the crags and fields glowing golden-green in the fading light, listening to the gentle clack of Mrs. Drabble's knitting needles keeping time with the rhythm of the wheels. Then the train rounded a bend, and I saw the ocean stretched out before us. I had been surprised when Mrs. Drabble had mentioned Grimly's location, for Matron had neglected to tell me it was on the coast. I had always held a special affection for the seaside, for it was tinged with happy memories of sea-bathing and fairground rides and toffee-apples on sticks. The seaside of our Brookvale excursions was gentle and welcoming, tamed by commerce, a place of perpetual holidays. But this ocean outside the window looked altogether different – wilder, more free, more dangerous. But perhaps in time, I hoped, I would grow to love it too.

Mrs. Drabble glanced up, catching sight of the distant stripe of blue-grey water. She sighed with contentment. "Ah," she said, "it lifts the heart to see the sea again, that it does. Whenever I'm away from it I miss its roar. And the air smells different by the sea – cleaner, more refreshing. I'm sure it does a body good; maybe it'll give you a little color in your cheeks."

I felt myself blushing, and ducked my head.

"Not far to go now," Mrs. Drabble continued, oblivious to my embarrassment. "The line turns back inland for a while, for Grimly station is a good three miles from the village itself. Is someone meeting you?"

"I'm to stay tonight at the inn, then travel to Greythorne Manor in the morning," I said. "I believe the innkeeper is sending someone to collect me from the station."

Mrs. Drabble nodded approvingly. "The Grimly Arms is a nice enough place," she said, "and Arthur Greenslade and his wife are decent folk – you'll come to no harm there. But I do wish you'd reconsider going to Greythorne Manor, my dear. I fear no good will come of it."

"Tell me, please: why do you speak so?"

Mrs. Drabble opened her mouth to answer, but was cut short by the rattle and screech of the brakes as the train drew into Grimly station. As it slowed to a halt we rose and collected our belongings; the moment had passed. I carried only my small carpetbag, for I had few personal possessions, and my clothes and books were all in my trunk, stowed in the goods van. But Mrs. Drabble was juggling a large covered basket, a traveling bag and several brown paper parcels. I took the basket and passed the parcels down to her as we disembarked.

"Eh now, that's a grand help," she said. "You're a good girl, Nell. It's such a shame to see you going to a place like Greythorne. You're sure you won't come home with me? We could find you some work on the farm until you're able to get yourself another position. And the Greenslades are always looking for girls to work at the inn. It'd be a step down, perhaps, but there are plenty of opportunities in Grimly for a smart, hard-working girl like you – you don't have to do this, you know."

Her repeated insinuations had begun to rattle my already-frayed nerves, and I very nearly accepted her offer. But I gritted my teeth and held firm, thinking of little Sophie Greythorne. I knew what it was to be motherless, to have no one to run to with life's joys and troubles, and I would not wish it on any child. If it was within my power to make even the smallest amount of difference to this little girl's lonely life – and how lonely it must be, if all the stories about Greythorne Manor's isolation were true! – then I had a duty to try. For if Mrs. Drabble thought it an unsuitable home for me, a grown woman, how much worse might it be for a child? Besides, the Professor was expecting me, and should I fail to appear it would reflect terribly on Matron and the other Brookvale staff, who had all been so good to me. So I shook my head, though not without some regret.

"You're very kind," I said, "but I cannot. I must go to Greythorne Manor tomorrow as planned."

"Very well." Mrs. Drabble squeezed my arm kindly. "I understand. But if you change your mind, our door is always open. Lark Hill Farm, on the Grimly–Little Norton road. You can't miss it. Ah, there's Arthur Greenslade over there." She waved at a plump, middle-aged man who was conversing with the station-master. When he saw her he broke off his conversation and came towards us.

"Elsie," he said with a broad smile. "Back from town? And how's your Katie?"

"Evening, Arthur," Mrs. Drabble said. "She's doing very well, thank you. Now, I believe this is the young lady you're looking for."

"Miss Featherstone?" He tipped his hat. "Arthur Greenslade. Welcome. You're bound for Greythorne Manor, I hear?" His tone was jovial, but he and Mrs. Drabble exchanged a glance, which added to my discomfort.

"Yes, sir, that's correct."

"Well then, you just come along with me, and the missus'll find you a soft bed and a hot meal. It's a long journey from the city, particularly for them as aren't used to it. Can we give you a lift, Elsie?"

"Nay, thank you, Arthur. That fool husband o' mine should be along shortly. I'll just wait here."

"Thank you for your help, Mrs. Drabble," I said. "It was very nice to meet you."

"And you too, love." She patted my shoulder. "Now, don't you forget my offer. If anything goes amiss at Greythorne you're always welcome to stay with us for as long as you need. I'll pray for you every night, my dear."

I smiled, both comforted and disquieted. Her offer of hospitality was generous, and it was kind of her to include me in her prayers, but her reluctance to tell me why I would need such intervention unnerved me. I waved to her as I rounded the corner of the little station waiting-room, and she waved back, but her eyes were troubled.

Chapter 2

I followed Mr. Greenslade to his cart, where my trunk had already been stowed, my head spinning. I felt suddenly very tired; although I had thought myself a grown woman, perhaps I was really little more than an overwhelmed child in a big and frightening world. I climbed into the cart and Mr. Greenslade clicked to the horses. We lurched out of the station-yard and onto a chalky white road that turned back toward the coast; already I could hear the roar of the sea and smell its salty tang.

"Have you lived in Grimly long?" I asked Mr. Greenslade, after we'd been trotting along for a goodly time. I wasn't normally one to initiate conversations, but I hoped it might distract me from my increasing unease.

"Aye, all my life," he said. "I were born and bred here. My father ran the inn, just like his father before him. Grimly were a prosperous little town back then, full of fishing boats. Eh, it were a grand sight, seeing them all lined up at the jetty of an evening. But then the fish stocks began to dwindle, and so did the boats, and the people followed. Now there's naught that go out of a night but one or two craft, crewed by men who'll be fishing this reach till the day they die. Our town's not what it was, but it's still a grand enough place to live, and I wouldn't want to be anywhere else. The sea is in my blood." He sat back, satisfied after this voluminous speech, and I tried to think of a response. Thankfully I was spared the endeavor, as the cart crested a rise and a pretty little village spread out before us.

"There you have it," Mr. Greenslade said proudly. "That down there is Grimly, and a lovely town she is too, even if I do say so myself."

I had to agree, for the cluster of whitewashed cottages set atop a small bay glowed like diamonds in the sunset. A few houses already had lights in their windows, and the overall effect was cozy and welcoming. I was enchanted.

The road began to slope down, and I could see that the village was nestled into the lowest point of a giant scoop in the land. The town opened out onto a beach and quay, which I presumed was the point of departure for the fishing boats Mr. Greenslade had mentioned, but on either side the coastline rose into chalk-white cliffs. Grimly Bay was the only sheltered spot for miles; it would be a bleak voyage indeed along this coast for any ship in danger of foundering.

"This here were once a favored spot for smugglers dodging the Revenue men," Mr. Greenslade said, "though that were long ago. It's a quiet, law-abiding place now."

It certainly sounded a pleasant-enough corner of the world in which to make a home. I had a feeling I could be happy there.

"And that," Mr. Greenslade continued, as we turned into the town's sloping main street, "is Greythorne Manor." He pointed down the wide thoroughfare, which dropped through the village all the way to the sea. I peered along the line of his hand, and suddenly understood why it was impossible to reach the Manor after dark.

The main street ran between two lines of whitewashed, slate-roofed houses, right down to the wharf. Away beyond the quay stretched the wide expanse of Grimly Bay, its white-tipped waves rolling relentlessly toward the shore, inhabited only by a rocky island. And atop this isle perched an old stone mansion, cold and desolate: Greythorne Manor. I shivered. Even at this distance the house appeared dark and foreboding, with no lights shining in any of its many windows. The dark stone – perhaps quarried from the very roots of the island on which it stood – reflected no warmth; it seemed to absorb the late-afternoon sunlight as a sponge absorbs water. Around the foot of the island the sea crashed and foamed against jagged rocks. The way was clearly treacherous, and only a fool with no care for his life would attempt such a crossing after nightfall.

Mr. Greenslade may have sensed my mood, or perhaps the sight of the Manor had the same effect on him as on me, for he shuddered. "'Tis a sad, lonely old place, right enough," he said. "No place for a child, and no place for a young lady such as yourself. There's queer goings-on there, it's said."

"I don't understand," I said. "Mrs. Drabble said the same thing, but she wouldn't tell me what they were."

Mr. Greenslade shrugged. "There's naught to go on but rumor and superstition," he said. "And maybe it's nothing but idle chit-chat started by people with more time than sense. All isolated old places get tales spun about them." But it sounded to me as though he was trying to convince himself. "Then again," he continued, "Elsie's a truthful woman; she likes a gossip, as all women do, but she would never put about falsehoods. She were good friends with Lucy Greythorne, though the young mistress could've been her daughter, and was devastated when she died. But she never much cared for the Professor. If Elsie tells you to stay away from the Manor you'd best be heeding her."

"I can't," I said. "I've already accepted the position."

He shrugged and said nothing, just slowed the horse to a walk down the steep cobbled street. My momentary happiness at finding Grimly so pleasing had once again been shunted aside by profound disquiet, but I tried to dampen it as best I could. After all, as Mr. Greenslade had said himself, all isolated old places had tales spun about them. More than likely I'd find only a reclusive, grief-stricken man, a tad eccentric perhaps, living in complete ignorance of what the villagers were saying about him. Greythorne Manor was lonesome and imposing, to be sure, but I had no logical reason to fear it. I set my jaw, feeling my determination rising. I'd take this job, and I'd mold Sophie Greythorne into a bright, sociable young woman, and they would all see how wrong they'd been about the place.

The cart drew up in front of a cozy-looking inn set a few streets back from the waterfront, with a sign over the door proclaiming it the Grimly Arms. "Here we are, then," Mr. Greenslade said. "You hop down and go on in while I put the cart away. I'll take your trunk straight to your room, so you won't need to worry about it. The missus'll fix you up with a hot meal."

I did as he said, climbing down from the cart, careful not to catch my skirt on the step. I had only a few gowns – all drab browns and blues and greys like this one: sturdy, if not exactly luxurious – and although I could sew my own clothes quite capably, I did not wish to tear one. Mr. Greenslade passed my carpetbag down after me, then drove the cart into the inn yard, while I tentatively opened the door.

A bell jangled above my head, and I stopped and looked about me. The entrance opened straight into a warm, wood-paneled tap-room, with booths for drinkers tucked around the walls and long tables down the middle of the room for those wanting a meal. Behind the bar a merry-looking woman was wiping her hands on a red-and-white checked cloth. When she saw me she flung the cloth over her shoulder and hastened out from behind the counter, greeting me with a cheerful grin.

"Miss Featherstone, I presume?"

"Please, call me Nell."

"I'm Frances Greenslade. Welcome to Grimly."

"Thank you."

"Did you have a pleasant journey? You must be hungry. Sit yourself down and I'll fetch you a meal."

The food was rustic but hearty, and there was plenty of it – a thick lamb stew with carrots, peas and new potatoes swimming in gravy, served with a hunk of fresh homemade bread. I hadn't realized how famished I was until it was set before me, for although I had eaten a packet of sandwiches on the train, that seemed days earlier. My stomach growled in appreciation, and I hoped Mrs. Greenslade couldn't hear it, for such things didn't seem quite proper.

I finished my meal and sat back with a contented sigh. The world looked much rosier on a full belly, although I was suddenly very tired.

Mrs. Greenslade must have noticed I was nearly falling asleep at the table, for as she collected my plate she gave my shoulder a friendly pat. "Why don't I show you to your room?" she said. "I'll send one of the maids up with some hot water for a wash, and then you can rest. I know how long train journeys take it out of a person."

"Thank you, you're very kind." I rose, picking up my carpetbag. "I was told someone from Greythorne Manor will be coming to collect me in the morning?"

"Aye," Mrs. Greenslade said, "that'll be old Jonas. But he'll have to wait for the tide, so he probably won't arrive before lunchtime. You're welcome to come to church with us at nine if you wish."

"Thank you. That would be lovely."

"Sleep well then, my dear, and I'll wake you tomorrow."

"Good night."

It was far earlier than my normal bedtime, for the sun had been down only an hour or so, and it was my routine of an evening to spend a few hours reading or sewing. But the long journey had worn me out; as

I collapsed into the soft featherbed even my worries about the morrow were insufficient to keep me from drifting into a deep, dreamless sleep.

Chapter 3

It seemed but a few minutes before I was awakened by a knock at the door and the landlady's friendly voice. I rubbed my eyes, groaning, for although I had slept well I still felt weary. Hauling myself out of bed, I washed and dressed in my Sunday best – which, truth be told, wasn't so very different from my everyday gown – and my only hat. Breakfast was on the table downstairs, but I ate alone. Any other guests there must still have been fast asleep, and although I could hear the kitchen maids, I didn't see them.

Mrs. Greenslade came in as I was finishing my meal, looking resplendent in a dark blue gown and towering hat. Her husband, following close behind her, had been scrubbed until his face shone.

"Good morning, miss," he said. "How did you sleep?"

"Very well, thank you."

We walked together in the direction of the church, which was only a few streets away from the inn. "Tell me," I said with sudden curiosity, "will Professor Greythorne be in church today?"

Mrs. Greenslade laughed. "Him? Not likely. The last time he darkened the door of a church was at his poor wife's funeral, though if you believe the stories he needs it more than most. He wouldn't even allow poor Lucy a decent burial in the graveyard here, though she were Grimly born and bred – he took her back to that island of his. If there was ever a place to keep a body from eternal rest that would be it, but he couldn't be prevailed upon, no matter how strongly the vicar and the churchwardens put their case."

The church was a quaint little stone edifice dating from the earliest days of Grimly's settlement. It was well attended, and, as is the case in small country parishes, the Greenslades knew everyone.

"Miss Sarah Persimmon, may I present Miss Nell Featherstone?" Mr. Greenslade said, introducing me to a thin, sharp-faced woman seated behind us. "Miss Persimmon is the schoolteacher here and has been for many years."

"Pleased to meet you."

"And you. What brings you to Grimly?"

"Miss Featherstone is to be Sophie Greythorne's governess," Mr. Greenslade interjected, before I could say a word.

"*Oh*," Miss Persimmon said, her eyebrows rising. She shot a glance at Mrs. Greenslade, but I pretended not to see. Every subsequent introduction was the same; the friendly, welcoming smile, then the shuttering of the eyes, like a blind dropping, at any mention of Greythorne Manor. I was glad when the service started, for my nerves had returned tenfold, and I took comfort in the familiar prayers.

Afterwards, I was introduced to the vicar, Mr. Davis. He, too, looked startled when I mentioned Greythorne Manor, and grasped my hand in apparent concern. "I don't wish to alarm you," he said, "but accepting this position may be ill-advised. Greythorne Manor is an eerie place, and the Professor a notable eccentric. It's not for me to trade in rumor and gossip, but I do wish you'd reconsider."

"And what of Sophie Greythorne, sir?" I asked, for I was growing tired of the vague but earnest exhortations. "Would you leave a child alone in such an environment?"

The vicar sighed, then seemed to resign himself. "I see you will not be easily dissuaded, Miss Featherstone," he said. "You will be in my prayers."

After church, we returned to the inn and sat down to a sumptuous Sunday luncheon of roast beef, Yorkshire pudding and home-grown vegetables. I was already growing fond of the Greenslades, and would be sorry to leave. But Greythorne Manor wasn't so very far away, and it was possible I might be able to make regular trips back, perhaps to attend church on Sundays, even though the Professor seemed so against the practice. I wondered when his man Jonas would arrive.

I was sitting in the Greenslades' little parlor, which opened off the inn's large broad-beamed kitchen, when I heard the bell on the main door tinkle and Mrs. Greenslade's voice saying, "Ah, Mr. Jonas. Come in." I rose and returned to the tap-room, unsure if I felt nervous or excited.

"Nell, my dear," Mrs. Greenslade said when she saw me. "This is Mr. Jonas. This is Nell Featherstone, Sophie's new governess."

Jonas was neither tall nor handsome, with a visage not improved by his sour expression. He did not take my proffered hand, but merely looked me up and down then grunted. "You'll do, I s'pose," he said, then he turned and walked back out the door. I stared at Mrs. Greenslade in amazement.

"Don't you mind him," she said. "He's not one for talking, is Jonas. He's already collected your trunk and taken it to the boat. You'd best be going, for he's not the most patient of men."

"Thank you for your hospitality," I said. "I'd hoped to be able to farewell Mr. Greenslade as well."

"Ah well, never mind that," she said. "I'll pass it on to Arthur, and in any case, I hope we see you again soon. You'll need Jonas to row you to the mainland, of course, but he comes over periodically to replenish the house's supplies, so maybe he'll allow you to join him one of these days."

"I hope so."

My carpetbag was already packed and waiting in the parlor, so I collected it, pulled on my overcoat – for although it was only autumn, the sea wind was chill – and joined Jonas outside. I think I had expected some sort of conveyance, for I was rather surprised when he instead strode off down the street toward the quay. I hurried after him, turning once to glance back at the Grimly Arms, where Mrs. Greenslade was standing, waving her red-and-white tea-towel. But when I turned again she had vanished, and an impatient bark from Jonas made me start and hurry onward.

A small wooden dinghy was tied up to the quay, bobbing gently on the waves, my trunk resting in its bows. I was glad there was little breeze to speak of, and the bay was relatively calm; I had never been in a boat on the sea before – though I had once paddled on a pond during a Brookvale outing – and the last thing I wanted was to embarrass myself by becoming sick.

"Get in, then," Jonas snapped, hauling the boat closer to the quayside. I had not the faintest idea of how to board a boat without assistance, so I could only look at him helplessly. He sighed in exasperation and lowered himself expertly into the unsteady craft, holding out his hand to me. This gentlemanly grace seemed to cost him dear, for it was clear I tried his patience. Nevertheless, I was glad of the help, and was able to embark without incident.

Jonas settled into the middle of the boat and busied himself with unshipping the oars and untying the rope from its bollard. I perched where he told me, in the stern – presumably to balance the weight of the trunk – taking deep breaths of sea air to calm myself. This bobbing about on the waves like a cork felt highly unnatural, but Jonas clearly saw nothing odd about it.

As the oars caught the water and the boat pulled away from the wharf I took the opportunity to study Jonas. Although we were facing each other, he did not look at me. But, not wishing to be caught staring, I alternated surreptitious glances with fixing my eyes on the rocky island that was our destination.

Jonas was older than I had expected; he must have been at least fifty. He wore his gray-flecked brown hair long, the unkempt locks almost brushing his shoulders, and his nose was prominent and hooked like an eagle's beak. His eyes were as grey and hard as river pebbles, while his mouth had a distinct downward slant and his chin was unshaven. With Jonas as the village's representative of Greythorne Manor, it was no wonder all manner of stories abounded.

I wanted to ask him about the house, and the Professor, and Sophie, but I could see he was an unlikely conversationalist, and, truth be told, I was a little afraid of him. So I said nothing, just sat and listened to the squeak of the rowlocks and the thud and splash of the oars, as our destination grew ever closer and friendly little Grimly receded into the distance.

The sea began to get rougher as we neared the vicious ring of rocks that imprisoned the island, and I could not stifle an exclamation, for I feared we would be dashed to pieces.

"Are you sure you know the way?" As soon as the words were spoken I regretted them, for Jonas gave me such a sneering look that I felt about three inches high. And of course he would know the way, for hadn't Mrs. Greenslade told me he visited the mainland regularly to replenish supplies? I blushed at my foolishness, and resolved to keep my thoughts to myself for the rest of the journey.

It seemed to me, as one ignorant of the sea and its tempers, that there was no safe passage between the jagged rocks upon which angry waves crashed and foamed, but Jonas guided the boat expertly through, finding the only patch of calm water. I made sure I paid attention, though I didn't anticipate having to make such a crossing alone.

The rocky shore of the island now loomed up above us, dark and foreboding. We were too close to be able to see the house directly, but I could almost feel its presence, like that of some great crouching beast. The water was calmer now we were inside the ring of rocks, and my stomach, which had clenched itself in knots during the last treacherous phase of our crossing, began to settle. Now that the journey was nearly over, however, new worries crowded in on me.

Jonas pulled the boat into a calm little beach and helped me to disembark before unloading my trunk and hauling the dinghy far up out of reach of the tide. Then he hefted my trunk onto his shoulders and began to trudge up a narrow path, which I presumed led to the house. I was amazed he was so capable after such a voyage, for he was neither a young man nor a large one, but it was clear he was immensely strong. I grabbed my carpetbag, hitched up my skirts and hurried after him.

The island was wild, but not as bare as I had thought it from the mainland. The path – which was really little more than a rabbit-track, for no one had attempted to mark it out except through repeated traversing – wound its way through tufts of hardy grass and weedy bushes, all battered by the sea wind and salt spray, yet miraculously thriving. I would not have thought much could live in such an inhospitable place, yet nature seemed determined to prove me wrong.

Jonas set a fearsome pace, even with the trunk, and it was all I could do to keep up with him. The path rose steadily, for the house had been built at the top of the island. The wind, fresh, biting through my coat, and tangy with the smell of the sea, whipped my hair out of its neat bun and flung it into my eyes; my skirts tangled around my legs.

We crested a rise, and suddenly Greythorne Manor loomed before us. It was a sprawling, eerie old place, a true monstrosity, with a square, crenelated tower at each corner. The house looked like it had been designed by a child, with mismatched wings extending chaotically beyond the towers, at odds with the original structure. Its hulking stone walls and steeply-pitched roof lacked any sort of objective aesthetic beauty, yet it both dominated and conformed to the landscape around it. Even as the house soared over its rocky perch, lord of all it surveyed, yet so the island was infused into its very walls. I had never seen anything like it.

I stopped and stared for a moment, but Jonas must have noticed me pause, for he turned.

"Hurry up!" he snapped. "I haven't got all day!" It was the first thing he'd said to me since boarding the boat. I jumped and hastened after him.

The front side of the Manor – the side that, in any normal house, would open onto a broad carriage-drive – was the side that faced the mainland, and which I had observed the previous evening. But Jonas led me round to the back, the seaward-facing side, which was less grand, but to me no less imposing. Around the house grew a few tenacious trees, mostly pines, standing indefatigable in the face of wind and sea. Yet the greenery did little to render the house more welcoming, and the turf underfoot was rocky and uncultivated, with nothing growing but some tufty grass.

I followed Jonas to what was clearly the servants' entrance and through a narrow door. I was not surprised it was unlocked, for what need of security was there here? The door opened onto a long, narrow passage, dark but for a single lamp left burning to light the way: little light made it in from outside. The hallway led down to an enormous kitchen, which, to my surprise, was deserted. I realized I had not seen another soul besides Jonas since we landed on the island, yet a house of this size would surely require staff. Where was everyone? It was eerie to see the room that was ordinarily the heart of any home so desolate.

Jonas led me out of the kitchen and up the back stairs. I wondered whether I was to be given a room in the servants' quarters, which would be an insult even to the likes of me. I was, after all, a gentleman's daughter, even if my fortunes had taken a turn for the worse since my poor parents' passing. And really, it was no wonder Professor Greythorne could not attract a governess with better connections, for who would voluntarily submit themselves to such a situation?

I was working myself up into a riot of indignation, but it turned out to be ill-founded; Jonas led me into the family areas of the house and along a wide hallway, off which opened a number of doors. All were closed, and the dusty carpet and general air of disuse indicated these rooms were also free of occupants. Further along, the grand staircase opened down into a black-and-white tiled foyer. I wondered why we hadn't just come through the front door and up the main stairs – it would have been far shorter – and asked Jonas as much.

"The front door hasn't been used since the mistress died," he said. His voice was as gruff as usual, but if I didn't know better I would have thought I detected a hint of sadness. The man was certainly an enigma.

We continued along the hallway, then Jonas stopped and, divesting himself of the trunk, took a large ring of keys from his pocket and unlocked a door to his left.

"These are your quarters," he said. "The schoolroom and Mistress Sophie's bedroom are connected to them by an internal door. You may go to these areas, the kitchen, the library, the drawing room, the dining room and the garden; you're not to wander anywhere else. Is that clear?"

I nodded, biting my tongue so I wouldn't ask why.

The room was large, well appointed, and, most importantly to my mind, clean. Jonas deposited my trunk at the foot of the enormous four-poster bed.

"This do?"

"It's lovely, thank you." This was not a falsehood; the room was indeed pleasant, with the large windows affording a good view over the island and the sea.

"Dinner is at seven in the dining room," he said. "The Professor expects you to dress for it."

"Of course."

"Anything else?"

"When will I meet Sophie?"

Jonas shrugged. "She's probably in the schoolroom. If not, she'll be out roaming the island somewhere. She'll turn up. Just introduce yourself."

This seemed highly unorthodox to me – no wonder the girl was half-wild, with such an upbringing! – but I did not object. Jonas turned on his heel and left without a word. Really, the man was one of the rudest I'd yet encountered! And could I trust him? That was a question I could not yet answer; I hoped time would tell.

Chapter 4

After Jonas's departure I busied myself with unpacking my trunk and exploring my new living quarters. These proved to have everything I needed – ample space for my gowns and underclothes, an armchair, a small but serviceable writing desk, and a washstand and dressing table against one wall. Beyond the bedroom lay the schoolroom.

Unpacking took little time because my possessions were so few, so when I was finished I walked to the window, flung open the casement and thrust my head and shoulders into the fresh air. Leaning out as far as I could go, I let the wind whip through my hair. Below me the rocky island stretched out until it merged into the sea a few hundred feet from the manor. From this side of the house, looking away from the mainland,

I might have been the only person in the world. What could it possibly be like to grow up in such a place?

These thoughts naturally led me back to my young charge, and I wondered where I should find Sophie. The schoolroom was the first and most obvious place to look. I had already located the door that joined my bedroom to it; now I tried the handle and found it unlocked. I peered through, not wanting to startle the child by coming upon her unannounced, but the room was empty.

"Hello?" I called, opening the door wider and tentatively stepping through. The room had the strange hybrid air of a place belonging to a girl who was no longer a small child but not yet a young woman. Remnants of childhood still occupied various corners, like a gaggle of dolls perched on a shelf, and a rocking horse grazing by the far wall. But there was also an immense bookcase stuffed with all manner of volumes, and a large table where presumably we would take our lessons. The room was lit, like mine, by substantial windows that afforded a breathtaking view of the ocean, and there was also an ample open fireplace, which would make it snug in winter. Before the fire crouched an armchair, rocking chair and work table: the perfect place for reading, sewing or preparing lessons. It was a pleasant enough little room and would make a more-than-adequate schoolroom, if only I could locate my pupil.

Two more doors opened out of the schoolroom – one clearly led into the hall, and the other, opposite the one by which I had entered, presumably led to Sophie's bedchamber. It too was unlocked.

I opened it and went through, gently closing it behind me. "Sophie?" I called softly, but there was no reply, and at first I thought this room also deserted. It was not dissimilar to my own, with a large four-poster bed and picture windows, but it had the warmth that comes with being lived in. I walked over to the window, then heard a noise behind me. My heart pounding, I turned and, to my surprise, found a little girl sitting on the floor beside the bed, a book lying open at her side.

I had already begun to develop a mental picture of Sophie, but it was based only on the Professor's and Jonas's meager descriptions and my own imaginings, so it was hardly surprising that it turned out to be wrong. In my head she was a dark-haired, rosy-cheeked child, plump and healthy from spending most of her days outdoors, with a wild, independent streak that came from growing up in such a place without motherly oversight. But the girl on the floor was pale and wispy, with a bone structure as fine as a bird's and a complexion the color of milk. Her hair was fair, somewhere between blonde and brown, and her dark eyes were huge in her pale face, the effect accentuated by the black high-necked gown she wore.

If there was any trace of wildness about her it was not immediately apparent. She seemed unsurprised by my presence, as if odd things happened to her regularly; she simply looked at me and said nothing.

Not knowing what else to do, I sat down next to her on the floor. "Hello, Sophie," I said. "I'm Nell – I mean, Miss Featherstone – your new governess." It was not how I had anticipated being introduced to my charge.

She fixed those big brown eyes upon my face, but I felt that, although she was looking at me, she was seeing something else. Her skin was so pale as to be almost translucent; I fancied I could almost see the blood running through her veins. "Hello," she said with equanimity. "Tell me, how does the moon affect the tides? I would ask Papa, but he's busy."

I stared at her, taken aback. Thanks to Brookvale, I was amply equipped to teach English, German, French, history, geography, drawing, needlework and even music, but we had not focused on the natural sciences; it was not considered proper for young ladies. It was due only to my own reading that I was able to answer her question.

"It's because of gravity," I said. "The moon pulls the earth and attracts the sea towards it, causing high tides." It was a simplistic, layman's answer, and I hoped she would not probe further, but thankfully it seemed to satisfy her.

"I know all about the tides," she said, twirling a strand of hair idly round her forefinger. "I made Jonas tell me all about them, and how to get the boat through the big rocks. Papa thinks it's *so* secret, but *I* know." She gave me a shrewd look that I found not entirely comfortable; it seemed old beyond her years.

"What else do you like to read, Sophie?" I asked, picking up the book that lay on the floor – *Gulliver's Travels*. I was hoping to get back onto firmer ground.

"Everything," she said. She leaned in closer, with a confidential air. "It can be a bit lonely here sometimes," she said, "but I have lots of friends in my books. And I want to know *everything* about the world." Then she smiled, a beautiful, winsome smile that melted my heart, but left it aching.

"Well," I said, a turmoil of emotions thudding in my chest, "I'll be your friend now. You don't have to be lonely any more. And together we'll explore all the things you want to know and more besides. Would you like that?"

I had expected her to concur happily, having just confessed to her loneliness, but she simply shrugged in a non-committal way. "I don't really need a governess," she said. "I don't know why Papa suddenly thinks I do."

"Well then, you can just think of me as a new friend for now," I said, slightly upset by her dismissiveness. Nothing at Brookvale had prepared me for this.

She just looked at me under her eyebrows and shrugged again, as if to say *We'll see*.

"Do you get to play with other children?" I asked, wondering if she ever went to Grimly with Jonas or her father. She shook her head, her hair swinging.

"I don't really leave the island," she said. "Not since Mama died. Once I went to the village with Jonas, but the other children laughed at me and called me names. They're hateful; I don't want to play with them!" Her bottom lip quivered, her brow creasing into an obstinate frown. I wondered if her father had spoiled her, or if this behavior was simply the result of spending too much time alone. It would probably take her a while to adjust to having a near-constant companion.

"I say, Sophie," I said as an idea occurred to me, "I haven't had the chance yet to see much of the island, apart from the way up from the boat. Why don't we go for a walk and you can show me around?"

She seemed to think about the proposition for a moment, chewing her bottom lip. "I don't feel like walking right now," she said. "I'm reading. You may go. I'll call you if I need you."

This could not be borne, and I think she could see from my face that she had overstepped the mark. "Now, look here, young miss," I said, "I am not your servant, and it is not your place to give me orders. Your father has asked me here to aid you in your education, and I intend to do so to the best of my ability. But I will not tolerate impertinence or laziness. Do you understand?"

She nodded, refusing to meet my eyes, and scrambled to her feet. I rose more slowly, for I had not her flexibility, and it had been a long time since I last sat on the floor.

"Fetch your boots," I said, noticing she wore only stockings. "And your coat; the wind is cold."

She stared at me again, clearly unused to being commanded in such a fashion, then did as I had requested, though she wore a sullen expression. Her boots were rather scuffed, but her dress and coat were neat and clean, if patched in places.

"Who washes and mends your clothes?" I asked, for it was yet another mystery in this apparently servant-less house.

She shrugged. "Jonas."

I felt my eyebrows rising in surprise. "But I thought Jonas was your father's assistant?"

She shrugged again, seemingly unbothered by the whole thing. "He is. But he does other things too. He cooks and cleans a bit, because we don't have a housekeeper any more."

"Why not?"

"I don't know. I think we used to have one for a while, but she left. And then we didn't get another one, so Jonas had to learn to cook, because Papa can't and they won't let me near the stove." She sniffed, clearly not approving of this decision. "I know I could cook if they let me. I'm good at lots of things."

"I'm sure you are. Are you ready to go?" She nodded. I reached for her hand, but she scuttled away from me.

I followed her downstairs and through the big, deserted kitchen out into the garden, such as it was. There was little to delineate the formal beds from the island's encroaching wilderness, though I deduced from the squares of rotting wooden sleepers that there might have been a kitchen garden there at one time.

The fresh air appeared to have an electrifying effect on the child; she dashed ahead as if possessed, her hair streaming out behind her. "Sophie, wait!" I called, but I had to repeat myself several times before she slowed down. When I reached her she was standing, arms folded defiantly, her expression oozing resentment. I even fancied I caught a barely concealed roll of the eyes.

"Young ladies do not dash about so," I chided, remembering Miss Sims, the Brookvale etiquette mistress, and how she had drilled such points of decorum into us. I could only suppose Sophie had never had such things pointed out to her, and she seemed less than enthused by their revelation.

"*I'm* not a young lady!" she said. "Let's play hide-and-seek. You're it!" She shoved my shoulder rather roughly, stuck out her tongue – which, I confess, left me speechless with shock – and dashed off again, vanishing from sight before I could admonish her.

I briefly considered returning to the house, but I could hardly leave the child out there all alone – however much, at that moment, I may have wanted to – so I began to search, calling out her name. Although the island was not large, it was big enough that I could potentially be looking for hours if she was well concealed. I took a deep breath, trying not to let my ire show. This was not how I had envisaged spending my first day as a governess.

I began a rough circumvention of the island, making sure to look behind trees and rocks, but there was no sign of Sophie. A heap of boulders perched up on the clifftop seemed promising, so I clambered up to them, checking them over as thoroughly as I could but finding no clue. I was stretching my back and looking out to sea when I felt a hand pinch my waist.

"Boo!" Sophie yelled. I shrieked, jumping so high that I almost stumbled on the uneven ground. My heart was thudding so fast I feared it would burst from my chest. I rounded on the little imp.

"That's not funny, Sophie!" I snapped. But the little girl seemed to disagree, for she was laughing so hard she had to prop herself up against the rocks. I took her firmly by the elbow, set to march her back to the house in disgrace, but she wriggled from my grip like an eel and slipped between the boulders. I tried to catch her, but she had wormed her way into a little cavern underneath the piled-up rocks – perfectly child-sized, but far too small for the likes of me.

"Go away!" she said sullenly, her merriment gone.

I looked at the dusty ground and sighed; there was nothing for it. Hitching up my skirts, I kneeled in the dirt so I could peer into the cavern.

"Come now, Sophie," I said. "Enough of these silly games. Let's go back to the schoolroom. It will be time for dinner soon."

"I told you, I don't need a governess. I don't need *you*! And I'm not hungry!"

"Sophie, if this behavior persists I will have no choice but to involve your father." It was a threat I was reluctant to make, for I hadn't even met the Professor yet, and his impression of my competence would hardly be favorable if I confessed I had failed to control my charge on my first day. But my stock of ideas was rapidly diminishing.

"Go ahead and tell him, I don't care!"

I sighed. "Very well, then," I said. "If you're not hungry I guess I'll just have to tell Jonas to skip your dinner." I rose to my feet, brushing off my skirts, and turned back toward the house, but I had walked only a few steps before I heard a noise behind me. I turned and saw Sophie trailing reluctantly after me, her expression like a thundercloud. I wondered whether it was the threat of her father or of a confiscated dinner that had drawn her out, but I said nothing. As we walked on I tried to gauge the time from the fading light. Our little adventure had scuttled my plans for a sedate walk around the island; that would have to wait for another day.

On reaching the house, I was rather appalled to see how dirty we both were. Sophie's black gown had turned a dusty shade of grey, and although mine had been grey to begin with, my skirts were filthy and I could feel my hair falling in wisps about my ears. We would both need a good scrub before dinner, for although Sophie would eat in the schoolroom, I had to make myself presentable for the Professor.

"Right, young miss," I said as we passed though the overgrown kitchen garden, "it's nearly dinner time. We can go walking tomorrow instead." I was determined to assert my authority for once.

Sophie scowled, and looked like she was about to protest, but I set my lips firmly and stared her down, and eventually she acquiesced. We re-entered the house via the kitchen door and made our way back upstairs. Jonas had left Sophie's dinner on the table in the schoolroom, so I helped her wash away the worst of the grime and get into her nightclothes, then I sat beside her and watched her eat. She picked, sparrow-like, at her food, but eventually ate enough to satisfy me that she would not wake hungry in the night. When she was finished, she rose and took a large glass bottle filled with dark red liquid down from the shelf.

"I have to have my medicine now," she said.

"What for?" I asked, wondering if she was ill, but she ignored my question. I handed her a spoon and poured out a dose, which she drank without complaint, though from her grimace the taste was clearly unpleasant. I replaced the bottle, then tucked her into bed with one of her cloth dolls.

"Good night, Sophie," I said, but she simply rolled over to face the wall, her thumb in her mouth.

I turned the lamp down low and tiptoed back to my own chamber. It had been a strange day, but it was not over yet; I must tidy myself up as best I could, and go downstairs to meet the Professor. I thought it odd that he had not made himself available to greet me on my arrival, but then nothing about Greythorne Manor or its inhabitants was ordinary.

Chapter 5

Back in my chamber I found water on the washstand, and although it was cold, it was adequate for scrubbing clean my hands and face. I re-tied my hair into a neat bun, then stripped off my filthy gown and found one more presentable. I had no formal gown – for I certainly had not expected to be dining with the family – so I wore instead my Sunday best, which was a pretty, light blue dress that brought out the color of my eyes. I knew I was no beauty, but it concerned me little, and in fact in my present occupation I was glad of it, for a beautiful governess was apt to invite trouble and jealousy. In any case, when I surveyed the results in the looking-glass I thought them passable and, more importantly, respectable. Hurrying down the main stairs to the dining room, I heard a clock in the hallway chime seven. Although initially afraid of getting lost on the way, I found the room without incident.

The dining room was very pleasant, with a fire crackling merrily in the large grate, dispelling the chill of the autumn evening. A long, polished wooden table took up the center of the room, and at the head of it sat the Professor. He rose when he saw me enter, giving a little bow. He was formally dressed, and I suddenly felt my attire to be far less adequate than I had a few minutes earlier, but if he found any deficiency in my dress he was polite enough not to say so.

"Miss Featherstone," he said with evident warmth. "Welcome. I apologize for being unable to greet you personally this afternoon; I was engaged in an experiment that could not be neglected."

"I am pleased to meet you, sir," I said, "and please don't trouble yourself. Jonas provided for me more than adequately."

He laughed, a great booming laugh that I found almost infectious; I felt myself smiling automatically in response. "I doubt that," he said. "But Jonas is a good man, despite his lack of sociability. Please, have a seat." He pulled out a chair for me to his left and I sat obediently. In truth, I was somewhat taken aback. I had expected a notable eccentric, not this charming and, truth be told, rather handsome specimen.

The Professor was a man of middle years – I would hazard a guess at forty – but his hair was still jet-black, with only a few streaks of grey appearing at the temples. His moustache, which grew thick and luxuriant, was likewise not lacking in pigment. He had a distinguished, aristocratic nose and a firmly set jaw; the overall effect I found very pleasing. I had expected his eyes to be dark like Sophie's, but they were of the palest grey-blue, a striking feature in an otherwise tanned face. When he smiled I could recognize some similarity with his daughter, but I suspected she must take most strongly after her mother.

"I trust you are settling in well?" he asked, as Jonas entered bearing soup.

I nodded. "Sophie and I became acquainted this afternoon," I said. "She's a sweet child and seems keen to learn." I did not tell him of my real impressions, nor about the disastrous game of hide-and-seek, partly out of wounded pride and partly because I knew I would never win Sophie's trust if I went running to her father at the slightest infraction.

"She is a bright girl, no doubt," he said, "but she is undisciplined with regard to her studies. I would teach her myself, but I am much preoccupied with my work, and also I fear our temperaments would not allow for much progress." He gave a charming half-smile, little more than a faint crinkle around the eyes, which I took to mean that father and daughter both possessed the same fiery streak.

The soup, to my surprise, was delicious. I sipped some then asked a question I had been wondering about for some time. "What is your field of research, sir? I have been told you are eminent in the natural sciences?"

The flattery seemed to please him. "Eminent? Hardly. But I pride myself on working always at the cutting edge of the known sciences. Biology and anatomy are my specialties."

"Forgive me, sir, but I am mostly ignorant of those particular areas."

The Professor laughed. "You and much of the known world, I fear. It is a complicated science and unfit for polite conversation; suffice it to say that through my research I have made discoveries that, once published, will change humanity itself."

This sounded to me as if it verged on the heretical. I lowered my eyes to my plate and busied myself with eating. The Professor did likewise, and for some moments silence reigned.

"So tell me, Miss Featherstone, how do you like Greythorne Manor?"

"I like it very well, sir." This was not a complete untruth; there was something about the wildness of the place that was undeniably enticing, and the better-maintained parts of the house had comfort, some style – though sadly outmoded – and elegant proportions. "It is like nowhere else I have ever seen."

He laughed again, and a part of me was pleased I had the power to make him do so. "A very diplomatic answer," he said. "I know it must seem unusual to a young lady such as yourself, and that things are not done here in the most orthodox fashion. But unfortunately I fell upon hard times after my wife passed away, and so the house has not been kept in such good condition as it ought to have been."

"It still retains a certain … charm."

"You are very kind to say so." His eyes sparkled, and I felt myself blushing, though I had no reason to do so. The oddness of the situation made me bold.

"Forgive me for saying, sir, but you are not as I imagined you."

"I am not surprised. No doubt you heard tales in the village of the mad scientist who lives in a crumbling ruin on the island?"

"Something akin to that, yes."

"Well, a scientist I may be, but as for madness, I believe that falls upon others to judge. Do you think me mad?"

"No more so than most, sir." I was enjoying sparring with him, and it seemed the feeling was mutual, for his ready laugh burst forth again. Despite our short acquaintance there already existed between us an easy camaraderie. But I was nevertheless mindful that he was my employer, and any partiality on my part would be sure to jeopardize my position. Our association must remain professional, although part of me wondered if in time we could grow to be more akin to friends. While it would be highly presumptuous of me to expect such a thing in any other household, Greythorne Manor had so few occupants it seemed a shame not to be on good terms with them.

"I have to say, Miss Featherstone, that you surprise me as much as I do you," he said. "When I wrote to Brookvale requesting a governess I expected the kind of meek, bespectacled wallflower I am told usually resides in such institutions, not a charming young lady such as yourself. Tell me, what is your history?"

The compliments were balm to my soul, due simply to their rarity, but I tried not to let them go to my head. "My parents were both carried off by the typhoid fever when I was a child, sir, and so I grew up at Brookvale."

"So you have no living family? No one to protect your situation in life?"

"No, sir. After my parents died there was a search for relatives, but none were found. So I'm afraid I must fend for myself."

"How unfortunate. I too lost my dear mother when I was but a boy of fifteen; I know how impossible it is to reconcile such a loss. It is a cruel God indeed who would snatch a mother from her child in such a way." He paused, seemingly lost in memory. "Well, I hope you will consider Greythorne Manor your home now, and will be with us for some time to come."

"Thank you, sir, that is very kind."

The second and third courses passed in cheerful discourse; I sensed the Professor was happy to have another person to talk to, for I could not imagine Jonas to be the most engaging of conversationalists. The latter was, however, an excellent cook, and my opinion of the manservant improved further as the meal progressed.

When the last course had been cleared, the Professor escorted me to the hall, for I had expressed an inclination to return to my chamber. With only the two of us present it seemed ridiculous to observe the usual after-dinner customs of ladies withdrawing and the party reuniting over the tea tray. I thanked the Professor for his hospitality, feeling slightly giddy, though I had not partaken of the wine.

"My pleasure, Miss Featherstone, and I look forward to many more such meals and conversations," he said. "I find my digestion much aided by the addition of a handsome and erudite dining companion."

"Good night, sir."

"Good night."

I returned to my room and readied myself for bed, intending to read, but as I clambered into the four-poster I felt my foot brush something cold and rather slimy. Then, to my horror, the bedclothes began to move. I leaped from the bed, pressing my hand to my mouth to stifle a scream, and flung back the covers. A large, greenish toad blinked up at me from the middle of the sheets, then, with a flying leap, landed squarely on the flagstones. Slightly hysterical with relief, I began to giggle in a rather crazed fashion before pulling myself together and fetching the coal scuttle. I managed to coax the errant beastie in, then crept downstairs, unbolted the kitchen door and released it into the garden.

As I made my way back to my chamber I contemplated suitable punishments for wicked little girls who played tricks on their elders. But I could not help smiling in spite of myself, remembering how, years ago, I and several of my Brookvale fellows had done something similar to our dormitory mistress, Miss Blaxland – only we had used the enormous spider Louisa Brackenridge had found in her boot that morning. The poor woman's screams had woken the entire household, and Matron had spoken rather sternly to her, which had given us great enjoyment. And no punishment subsequently meted out had ever made us regret the offense.

Returning to bed – after checking it was free of any other unwelcome guests – I decided to leave my decision about Sophie's fate until the morning.

I opened my book and tried to read, but instead found myself turning the memory of dinner with the Professor over and over again in my mind. I found I could picture his face without effort: the ready smile and sparkling blue eyes; the affable laugh. Perhaps I had been brought to Greythorne Manor for a reason – to help this poor man and his daughter recover from their loss. And could it be possible that, in doing so, I too might find the family I had always longed for? Such dreams were ridiculous fantasies, I knew, but I could not help pandering to them just a little. Eventually, after seeing I had read the same page of my book multiple times without comprehension, I blew out the candle and snuggled down into the feather bed, cursing myself for a fool, but smiling as I did so.

Chapter 6

I slept soundly, although deep in the night I was awoken momentarily by a sound – a sharp thump and a cry – which seemed to come from very far away. Dazed and groggy with half-remembered dreams, I rolled over and fell asleep again, thinking it must have been the wind. In the morning I thought nothing of it.

I had left the curtains on my window open, for I suspected that without the early light to wake me I would otherwise sleep until mid-morning. As it was, the growing daylight and the cries of the seabirds roused me around eight o'clock. I stretched luxuriously in the massive bed, reveling in its size and softness, then sat up and swung my feet to the floor.

Upon examination I discovered that Jonas had left a covered jug of hot water outside my door, and silently blessed him. I performed my ablutions and dressed, then carried my books into the schoolroom, for today Sophie and I would begin our lessons.

I found breakfast for two laid out on the schoolroom table, but no sign of my charge. Setting down my books, I knocked gently at her door then entered, only to discover her still asleep.

"Sophie," I called, gently shaking her shoulder. "Time to get up." She groaned and rolled over, pulling the pillow over her head, but I was insistent. Eventually, with much grumbling on her part, I managed to coax her out of bed, where she stood barefoot and scowling on the rug, her thin arms folded across her chest.

"Can you wash and dress yourself?"

She glared at me scornfully. "I'm not a little child."

"Very well," I said, resisting the urge to tell her to stop behaving like one, "do so and then join me in the schoolroom for breakfast. And don't dawdle."

As I sat down at the table to await her, I reflected on what a strange life this girl must have led, which perhaps accounted for some of her less endearing qualities. She seemed to be a bright little thing underneath all that sullenness, but she had evidently been left to her own devices for far too long, and it was clear to me her upbringing was sadly lacking. I had read once that all brilliant men were relentlessly single-minded, and I suspected her father fitted this mold. Although he clearly loved his daughter, I wondered if he was fully cognizant that in a few short years she would be a woman grown and having to make her own way in the world. I had no knowledge of the Professor's financial circumstances, nor was it any of my business – he hopefully had enough money to pay my wages, and that was where my concern began and ended – but it was highly likely Sophie would either have to marry well or, like me, support herself in some way, and for both these paths she would require a good education and refinement of character. Her father had done her no favors by allowing this neglect of her development to continue for as long as he had, and I was sure poor Lucy Greythorne would be turning in her grave if she could witness it. It was clear I had my work cut out for me if Sophie were to become a young lady of credit to her name.

The object of my thoughts reappeared at that moment, washed, brushed and adequately dressed; she had even managed to fix her own hair, which surprised me. I spooned some porridge into a bowl as she seated herself at the table, and set it in front of her. "Here," I said, "eat up. I'm sure it will do you good. Did you sleep well?" I was asking out of genuine concern rather than convention; she looked pale and drawn, and had dark circles under her eyes. She shrugged wordlessly.

"Answer my question, Sophie," I chided gently. "It's impolite to ignore someone who addresses you."

"I slept tolerably," she said, her words directed at her porridge rather than me, "but I had the most awful nightmares."

"I'm sorry to hear that." I myself had slept so soundly I had not heard any cries of distress from her quarters. "Do you have nightmares often?"

She nodded. "Almost every night." How odd, I thought, filing this fact away to mull over later. I was glad to see, however, that her troubled night had not disturbed her appetite; she finished her porridge with gusto and started on bacon and toast, and afterwards seemed the better for it.

"Did *you* sleep well?" she asked as we sat sipping tea. From the look in her eyes it was clearly a loaded question.

"Why yes, thank you," I said with practiced equanimity. "Nothing disturbed me at all."

"Really?" She sounded disappointed.

"Yes, indeed."

"Oh. That's ... good." I was glad to hear my response had had the desired effect; she had clearly been looking for a reaction. I had the feeling I would not have any similar trouble from her again.

"What are we to do today?" she asked eventually.

"Well," I said, "today we'll begin our lessons. From now until luncheon we shall study geography and history. In the afternoon, if the weather permits, we can go for a walk around the island, and then I think we shall focus on art and music. Do you play the piano?"

"A little. I believe Mama was beginning to teach me, but I don't really remember much. We have a piano in the drawing room, but it hasn't been used for a long time." She paused as Jonas entered to clear away the breakfast things.

"Thank you, Jonas," I said as he loaded up the tray, but he merely grunted. The household arrangements were still passing strange to me, and I wondered again why the Professor didn't simply employ more servants. But perhaps he could not afford it – after all, he had said last night he'd fallen on hard times recently – or, more likely, he could not find anyone prepared to come. The tales and superstitions surrounding Greythorne Manor in the village would surely mean local help was all but impossible to come by.

"Very well," I said, opening my books and spreading out an atlas in front of us. "Let's start with geography."

"Must we? It's so *boring*."

"Yes, Sophie, we must. And it's not boring, not really. Think of all the adventures the early explorers had."

She sighed audibly, but gave no further resistance. We spent the morning tracing the major trade routes, learning of the traffic in spices, gold, ivory, tea, silk and other exotics, venturing across the wide oceans to the warmer climes of the New World and back again. We also dropped in and out of history, charting the rise and fall of empires, and though it was a rather unorthodox method of teaching – and I was unsure the Brookvale mistresses would approve – almost against her will Sophie seemed to become entranced by the feast of facts opening up before her. She had a naturally inquisitive spirit, always asking "Why?" – she was as much an explorer in her own way as Sir Francis Drake or Christopher Columbus or Vasco da Gama.

When the clock in the downstairs hall struck noon it seemed to me we had only been studying for a few minutes, rather than several hours. Sophie had lost some of her pallor, apparently energized by what was clearly a love of learning. Although I did not say so, I thought her existing knowledge vast for a child of her age, enhanced no doubt by her extensive reading, but it was patchy and would clearly benefit from more structured instruction. She remained resistant to those subjects that did not immediately pique her interest, and was apt to whine at such times, but as Jonas brought in the midday meal, I felt satisfied that we had made a good beginning.

Luncheon was hearty and satisfying, and I was once again surprised at Jonas's culinary prowess.

When we had finished I bade Sophie fetch her coat and did likewise myself, then we ventured downstairs and out through the kitchen door to begin our perambulation round the island.

The September day was crisp and clear, though a brisk wind blew in from the sea, chilling my bones in spite of the shining sun. "Where shall we go first?" I asked Sophie.

"This way," she said, pointing towards the seaward side of the island. "We can go right out to the point, then back round by the cove." She darted ahead of me, her hair fluttering in the wind. I caught her up when she stopped to look at some prettily colored moss on a rock, and took the opportunity to use our walk as a lesson in natural history. Sophie, warming to the spirit of the task, enthusiastically pointed to the stunted bushes and trees growing among the rocks, demanding to know the names of each and every one; science was clearly one of her passions. I answered as best I could, once again thankful that my own studies allowed me to hold forth on such a subject.

Before long – for the island was not large – we reached what Sophie had referred to as 'the point'. It was a small cape of rocks, the furthermost tip of the island, against which the sea pounded, throwing up cascades of wild salt spray. Sophie scrambled to the top of an enormous boulder, in spite of my exhortations to be careful; there she stood, with her arms stretched heavenward and her fair hair blowing like a banner behind her, leaning into the wind as if trying to embrace it. It was a strange, otherworldly pose for a little girl – or anyone, for that matter – and it reminded me yet again that Sophie was no ordinary gentleman's daughter, content to sit in a parlor with her sewing or her books, but a half-wild little imp in whose blood ran the thunder of wind and waves.

Standing beside Sophie – though on firm ground, for I possessed neither her youthful energy nor her disregard for dignity – I surveyed the seascape laid out before me. Like the child, I was fascinated by the Age of Discovery, and consequently I held in my heart a special affection for wild places, despite having seen few first-hand; there was something in the fierce untamed tumult of air and water that thrilled me. Out there, with naught before me but rock and sea, the salt air filling my lungs, I felt the lure of unknown possibilities that must have so captivated the early explorers.

Sophie seemed to sense my thoughts, for, jumping down beside me, she asked, "If we were to sail from here, how long before we reached the New World?"

"Oh, many weeks, I'm afraid. And besides, we have no boat."

"We could build one," she said, skipping beside me as we turned and continued our walk. "We could build a great big ship and sail far away from here."

"Would you really wish to leave, Sophie? Surely you would miss your father?"

She shrugged and went quiet. "Sophie," I asked, suddenly suspicious, "does your father treat you well?"

"Yes, of course." She sounded defensive.

"But you don't see him often?" I had already gathered her recent years had been spent much in solitude.

"He's very busy with his work. It's important."

"Of course."

"And he misses Mama," she added.

"You must miss her too?" Not for the first time, I wondered what had happened to Lucy; a long illness, perhaps, or maybe she had died in childbirth. Although the Professor had not mentioned another baby, such tragedies were not uncommon; a number of my Brookvale compatriots had lost their mothers that way.

Sophie nodded, then, apparently sick of this line of questioning, ran on ahead of me again. I followed more sedately, pondering the subtext of her words. The Professor had struck me as a personable, amiable man, possessing well-formed social graces and with none of the eccentricities rumor ascribed to him. Yet everyone coped with deep grief differently; I supposed it was possible he had been so heartsick as to be able to find distraction only in his work. But Sophie was grieving too – for, as I well knew, children feel such pain just as keenly as adults, though they are unable to express it as eloquently. My heart ached for the little girl, and, if I was brutally honest with myself, for her father also.

If Sophie was troubled by our conversation, however, she did not show it. For the remainder of our walk she darted back and forth like a puppy, bringing new treasures to show me – iridescent sea shells; knots of driftwood possessing faces like gnarled old men; stones worn smooth and round by the waves pounding them against the sand – before discarding them for something more novel. As we walked I began to develop a mental map of the island, which wasn't difficult, for it was mostly barren save for the grove of pine trees surrounding the house. Rabbit tracks traversed the boulders and scruffy vegetation, making it relatively easy to find a path.

Before long our way sloped down towards the little beach where I had arrived – only the day before, though it felt like months earlier! – but there was no sign of the boat. I mentioned this to Sophie with some puzzlement, and she grinned at me conspiratorially.

"In here," she said, beckoning me behind some large boulders. There, sure enough, was the little wooden dinghy, tucked safely away out of reach of even the highest tide; a second little boat lay beside it. "Jonas thinks it's a secret," Sophie said with a giggle. "But *I* know. He can't fool *me*."

We stood for a moment at the tide-line, idly tossing stones into the water. Across the bay Grimly stood, the afternoon sun glancing off the windows of the small white houses. I wondered if Jonas could be prevailed upon at some point to take me and Sophie there; I should like to introduce her to the Greenslades and Mrs. Drabble. I made a mental note to ask him the next time he went over for supplies.

We returned to the house by the same steep path I had trodden on my arrival. Back in the schoolroom, we divested ourselves of our outdoor clothing and I collected my music books before following Sophie downstairs to the drawing room.

The room was large and well appointed, though its opulent chairs and sofas were all swathed in dust covers. Similarly, the grand piano that stood to one side was also covered, but as I removed its sheet I could see it had been well cared for. Sophie opened the heavy drapes while I lit the lamps, for the afternoon light was growing weak. As I did so, I noticed a small portrait on the sideboard, showing a handsome young woman with fair hair and captivating dark eyes. Her resemblance to Sophie was unmistakable, and I concluded that this must be Lucy Greythorne.

Sophie sat down at the piano; I opened the lid halfway then sat beside her.

"Can you read music, Sophie?"

"A little."

We spent some time revising notes and learning scales; a necessary chore, though Sophie seemed to feel otherwise, and did not hesitate to communicate her boredom. After half an hour I began to teach her the simple French children's song *Au clair de la lune*, and was gratified to discover that she had a keen ear and a quick memory. By and by, however, she became restless and lacking in concentration.

"Might you play me something?" she asked me. "I should like to hear you play." She looked at me so beseechingly that I had not the heart to refuse her, even though I knew this was a ruse to allow her to shirk her lessons.

"Very well." The piece I chose was the first movement of Beethoven's *Moonlight Sonata*; its eerie, rumbling bass notes and funereal rhythms seemed peculiarly suited to this setting. It had been some time since last I played, but my fingers had not forgotten their old skills, and within a few minutes I was utterly absorbed. I was so engrossed in the music I failed even to notice the entrance of another person. It was only when the end of the movement was greeted by a slow clapping that I registered the Professor's presence.

"Bravo!" he said. I blushed and rose, flustered.

"I beg your pardon, sir," I stammered. "I was simply demonstrating to Sophie—"

"Pray, don't apologize," he said, with a smile and an incline of his head. "It is good to hear the instrument in use again. I trust it is in tune."

"Yes, sir." Considering its long disuse, the piano had actually held its tune remarkably well, which I could put down only to the room's relatively stable climate.

"I will not disturb you further," he said. "I only wished to congratulate you on your proficiency. It is a long time since this house had music in it." He turned to his daughter. "Listen and learn, Sophie. Although I doubt you will prove as accomplished as Miss Featherstone, you must work hard nevertheless. I trust you will do so?"

Sophie sat with her eyes downcast. "Yes, Papa."

"Good girl. I look forward to witnessing the results." He nodded to me, and withdrew. For a few moments after the door had closed behind him I stood staring at it, pondering his rather harsh words, but was drawn back to myself by Sophie rising from her seat.

"Do you wish to play again, Sophie?" I asked, but she shook her head. She looked tired and downcast; a mood quite different from the vitality that had infected her during the rest of the afternoon. I wondered whether her father's visit had prompted this decline in spirits, but in any case, we closed up the piano, and, drawing the drapes and blowing out the lamps, returned to the schoolroom. Once there,

Sophie curled into the armchair with a book, while I took my tapestry-work to the rocking chair. The rest of the afternoon passed in silent companionship, until Jonas arrived with Sophie's dinner and reminded me, as if I needed any such intimation, that I was once again expected to dine with the Professor. Sophie picked at her food, still silent and seemingly sad. I wondered if she was pining for her mother.

Dinner passed much as it had the previous night, with lively conversation, but I could not help but wonder at the Professor's rather callous treatment of Sophie earlier in the evening. Children required discipline, of course, but the Professor seemed to have little faith in his daughter's abilities – despite her obvious intelligence – and did not hesitate in making his feelings clear, though it seemed to me that Sophie would do better with encouragement than chastisement.

Having seen Lucy's portrait, however, I was beginning to make my own deductions about the cause of this conduct: the daughter was so like the mother that it must surely pain him to confront her, lest he be reminded of one so deeply loved and lost. But I could not excuse the behavior, however justified the circumstance that precipitated it, for I had seen the pain it inflicted on Sophie. The little girl loved her father, but how long could such love persist in the face of such coldness? And yet his regard did not appear to be abusive or cruel, but simply a method of self-protection enacted with no thought of the hurt inflicted upon the one to whom he denied affection. Involuntarily, I sighed.

"You are gloomy, Miss Featherstone?"

"Not at all, sir," I said, chiding myself for this lapse in countenance. "I'm simply a little tired. We walked right around the island today."

"It is beautiful, is it not?"

"It is indeed."

Glad that our conversation was now on more solid ground, I made sure to maintain a cheerful visage and, as the meal progressed, my mood began to lighten in truth. The Professor possessed a wicked sense of humor, and his anecdote about a local farmer who had somehow misplaced his pigs – which he swore was true – had me laughing until my stomach hurt.

"Thank you once again for a most enjoyable evening, Miss Featherstone," he said as we parted in the hall after the meal's conclusion. "I trust you too enjoyed yourself?"

"You know I did, sir. Good night."

"Good night, Nell," he said, with a depth of feeling that sent a tingle down my spine. He took my hand and pressed it to his lips; the unexpected sensuality of it made me gasp involuntarily. Then he smiled a little, raising his eyes to mine, and as our gazes met I felt my breath catch in my chest. I withdrew my hand as quickly as I could without giving offense and, blushing, hastened towards the stairs. When I reached the landing and glanced down, however, he was still there, watching me. He raised his hand in farewell and smiled, and I couldn't help but smile back.

Lying in my bed later, I replayed the scene over and over in my mind. This onslaught of feeling was new, but not unpleasant; but I was not so swept off my feet that I had forgotten my position or Matron's teachings. My first duty remained to Sophie, and I must be mindful of that, whatever regard I was developing for her father. As sleep claimed me, I wondered again what had happened to Lucy Greythorne, and what would become of her daughter.

Chapter 7

From then on, my days began to fall into a rhythm: Sophie and I would spend the morning with our books, learning history, geography, English literature, French and German. After luncheon we would venture outdoors if the weather permitted, or, on the wild, stormy days, play games or tell stories before the schoolroom fire. Afternoons were devoted to creative pursuits – music and the fine arts – and in fact Sophie excelled in everything she attempted. She clearly had her father's brilliance, and also a certain innate tenacity that meant she did not easily give up on problems she could not at first solve, although she took some convincing to attempt things outside her immediate area of interest. Her 'wildness' I soon found to be simply a child's over-exuberance coupled with a highly active imagination and a quick mind that, until recently, had been lacking in healthy stimulation. Now that her passions had been given a more constructive outlet her behavior also began to improve, and I had high hopes for her. She possessed enormous strength of character, in which I strove to instill sound principles. I had the feeling she would grow into a remarkable young woman, and I was becoming increasingly fond of her, as, I hoped, she was of me.

The autumn weather had been growing more and more miserable, and after a week of rain Sophie was restless at being kept inside. She had fidgeted all through our morning lessons, and as we finished our luncheon in the schoolroom she looked up at me imploringly.

"May we do something different this afternoon?"

I was inclined to be lenient, for she had been working well the past week and deserved a reward. "Of what were you thinking?"

"Let's go exploring!"

I glanced out the window, where the rain was cascading in sheets. "It's far too wet to go outside."

"I meant inside. I want to show you something."

I chewed my lip for a moment, but I was intrigued by the thought of exploring the house, for I had had little cause to go far beyond my rooms. I remembered Jonas's warning on the day of my arrival – which I assumed stemmed from the house's general disrepair – but with Sophie with me I would surely be safe enough. "Very well," I said. "Finish your luncheon."

*

After Jonas had cleared the plates, Sophie jumped up, grabbing my hand. "This way!" she said, dragging me out of the schoolroom door and down the gallery, the opposite direction to our usual way through the kitchen, and farther into the bowels of the house.

"Where are we going?" I asked.

"There are lots of ways in and out of here," she said, her eyes wide, not really answering my question. "Even Papa and Jonas don't know them all. But I'm an explorer, and I've discovered things. Things *no one* else knows."

I didn't know quite what to say to this, so I said nothing and simply let her lead me farther down the corridor. The passageway was dim, but Sophie seemed able to find her way almost by instinct. I, on the other hand, became hopelessly lost after we rounded several corners; the house was labyrinthine. More closed doors lined the hallway, and the sight of all those neglected rooms made me strangely sad.

"Where *are* we going?" I asked Sophie again after some time. She just grinned cheekily at me.

"You'll see," she said. "Do you like secret passages?"

"Well, I can't say I've ever been in one before."

"You'll like this one. You can sneak out at any time of the day or night and Papa will never know." I smiled to myself at the idea that I would want to sneak out in the middle of the night, but made sure she did not see.

The house was far bigger than it had looked from the outside, as if time and space were somehow stretched within, but perhaps it was simply my ignorance of its layout that provided this distortion. Without Sophie I doubted I would even be able to find my way back to my own room.

We came at last to one of the house's four towers, through which a spiral staircase curled. The passage skirted the edge of the tower, bending off at right angles to run along the perpendicular wall, but Sophie pulled me through the tower door into the stairwell. I stopped to peer out through the narrow slitted windows and could see little but stone and sea; this tower was evidently one of the two at the rear of the house. The staircase wound upwards, where I imagined it emerged onto the roof of the tower, and downwards, which was the direction in which we traveled. Upon reaching the ground floor, however, I noticed that the staircase, rather than terminating, continued down into the earth, bisected by a sturdy oaken door that stood open. The walls beyond the door were lined with tapestries bearing bleak hunting scenes in dark greens and browns.

"What's down there?" I asked, imagining some sort of cellar, or perhaps a medieval dungeon.

"That's Papa's laboratory," Sophie said, her eyes wide. "You mustn't go down there."

"Whyever not?"

But she simply stared at me and would not say another word. Had I not known better, I would have thought her afraid.

I assumed she would lead me out of the tower, but instead she took me through the oak door and a few steps down towards the cellar, then reached behind a tapestry and pressed a stone in the wall around her head height. To my astonishment, an entire section of the wall slid back; the tapestry now hid a gaping hole. The stones on this moveable panel were clearly false, but so well detailed as to be indistinguishable from their more solid fellows.

"In here," Sophie whispered, her eyes shining. Not without some hesitation, I followed her into the wall cavity, but was startled when the panel slid back into place, trapping us. I held my hand up to my eyes, but the darkness was so complete I was unable to distinguish its outline. I felt panic rising in my chest, and took some deep breaths to steady myself. Something brushed against my face and I jumped, but it was only a cobweb. Sophie's warm hand in mine was the only thing that kept the terror at bay. I hoped the passage would not narrow to a child's size, for then I would be in some difficulty.

"This way," Sophie said, sounding relaxed and confident. I felt her move and followed blindly.

"Are we inside the wall of the house?"

"Of course."

"How on earth did you find this?"

"I told you, I'm an explorer. Old houses always have secret passages – *all* the books say so."

In what was perhaps a sign of hysteria, I nearly laughed out loud at this absurd statement, for hadn't I too as a child been entranced by tales of mystery and adventure? I had explored Brookvale as thoroughly as I could, but it had yielded no enigmas, and certainly no secret passages. I could not decide if Sophie's childhood was to be pitied or envied.

Though we had been roaming the wall cavity all of ten minutes or so, to me it felt like hours. I peered ahead into the impenetrable blackness, trying to discern the faintest smidgen of light. I had completely lost my bearings.

"Not far now," Sophie said, but we continued for some time, until I began to fancy myself half-crazy, creeping along a dark, secret way with an eight-year-old girl as guide. I was meant to be the responsible adult; what would the Brookvale mistresses say if they could see me now?

Suddenly I was pulled up short by Sophie halting. "What's the matter?" I whispered. I know not why I was afraid of being overheard; perhaps it was the cloying effect of the darkness that made me speak in such a tone.

"Nothing," Sophie said, her voice sounding preternaturally loud as it echoed off the stones. "Here's the exit."

"How do you know?"

"We're at the corner of the wall," she said. "It's easier to tell with a candle, but I've been this way so many times now I can find it by feel. See?" She took my hand and pressed it against the wall, and, sure enough, I could feel it curving away. If she had not told me the turn was there I would have walked blindly on until I crashed face-first against the rock.

"The exit stone bears a mark," Sophie said, seemingly glad to share her secrets. "There's an *X* carved into it. At the corner, on the left-hand wall facing this way, count up five stones from the bottom and ten across." I did as she said, identifying the stones by feel and trying to suppress my skepticism. But all my doubts were quashed when, in the place she had identified, I felt a deep *X* beneath my fingers.

"I've got it."

"Good. Now just push on the stone. And stand back; it opens inwards."

I pressed my hand hard against the carving, feeling slightly ridiculous, only to leap back as, with a grinding sound, the wall moved as it had before. The only difference was this time it opened not into the tower, but to the outside. The rain had stopped, and I was bathed in the deep glow of the autumn afternoon. I stepped out of the cavity and breathed deeply, astonished at how relieved I felt to once again have the open air buffeting gently against my face.

"Really, Sophie," I said as she pressed another stone and the wall slid back into place, "it would have been far easier simply to use the door."

She giggled. "But far less fun." And whilst *fun* was not perhaps the term I would assign to our little adventure, I found I could not wholly disagree with her. She had dirt on her face and cobwebs in her hair, and I suspected I was similarly disheveled.

"Right, young lady," I said. "I think that's enough exploring for one day. Let's get cleaned up, then you can show me how your drawing is coming along."

She gave me a long-suffering look, but acquiesced without complaint. "It *was* fun, though, wasn't it?" she said as we re-entered the house.

"Yes," I said, with perhaps more enthusiasm than I'd intended, "it was."

Chapter 8

After the first few weeks, my evenings with the Professor became less frequent – much, I admit, to my regret – and I often took my dinner in the schoolroom with Sophie instead. He was, Jonas intimated, much absorbed in his work, and I found myself missing our conversations. Occasionally he would appear unexpectedly in the schoolroom, his presence having the same effect as it had that first day: Sophie became quiet, reticent and unresponsive, as if afraid of her father's censure. I tried to protect her as best I could, making sure he understood the remarkable depths of her progress, but this never elicited praise for my charge; his standards were exacting.

I had little free time, but once a month I was entitled to a half-holiday, and as it approached I wondered how I should spend it, for going to the mainland was not a possibility; Jonas had made it clear he had work to do around the Manor. The day, when it came, dawned grey and stormy, the low-hanging clouds holding the ominous promise of afternoon rain. After our morning lessons Sophie curled up before the schoolroom fire with a book; inspired, I decided to seek out the library, for I had read all my own books several times over.

I still found the layout of the house confusing, for, apart from our sojourn through the secret passage, I had had little cause to venture anywhere but the dining room, drawing room and kitchen. Wanting to challenge myself – and to seek scenery different from that of my normal routine – I decided to hunt for the library by a circuitous route, for I knew not exactly where it lay. I soon became lost in the Manor's labyrinthine passages, but it was a pleasantly thrilling kind of displacement, as if I was discovering things long hidden. Indeed, I wondered whether anyone ever frequented these halls any more, for they expressed a general air of abandonment, and the doors on every side were closed.

On impulse, I stopped and tried the handle of one of these rooms, expecting to find it locked, then gave an involuntary start of surprise as the brass knob moved beneath my fingers. Gingerly I peered through the doorway, half-afraid some Manor ghost would jump out to steal my soul. Shaking my head at my ridiculous notions, I squared my shoulders and ventured inside.

The room looked to have been a study at one time or another, but was clearly suffering from long disuse. All the furniture was covered in dust sheets, except the enormous leather-topped desk that lurked under the window. I went over to this monolith and perched myself in the covered chair behind it, staring out across its vast expanse back towards the door. The wood – mahogany, perhaps – had once been polished to a high sheen, but was now dull with age, and cracks as fine as spiders' webs were beginning to weave their way through the leather on the top. I felt a twinge of sadness that such a beautiful piece of furniture should suffer such neglect.

I rose from behind the desk and examined the rest of the room. There were several dusty bookcases, but these were locked and I could not find a key. I peered through the glass at the old forgotten tomes, and at the exotic-looking trinkets that lay on the shelves. Then, in the reflection, I caught a man's face staring back at me.

I started in fright and whipped around, but realized it was only an old portrait glaring from the far wall. Laughing at myself from sheer relief, I crossed for a closer look. The man in the picture was elderly and quite severe-looking; the artist had deftly captured the lines around his eyes and mouth that spoke of a wrathful temper. I wondered who he was – perhaps some distant ancestor of the Professor's? It occurred to me that I did not know how or why the Professor had come to Greythorne Manor, or whether it was even his ancestral seat, and reminded myself to ask him.

The eyes of the room's former occupant seemed to follow me wherever I stood, and I felt increasingly unsettled; in any case, there was little else to see. Returning to the hallway, I closed the door on the dismal chamber, leaving it once again to its solitude.

I tried several more doors as I went, but these were locked; all my romantic ideas of exploration were being decidedly deflated. I was now in a wing of the house unfamiliar to me, and was not quite sure of my bearings. If I could get to a room with a window, I could at least discover which side of the Manor I was on. I tried another door, hoping it would be unlocked, and, to my surprise, it was.

It was a bedchamber, and its décor was decidedly feminine. Unlike in the other rooms, none of the furniture was covered. The four-poster bed was trimmed with a ruffled canopy and valance, its coverlet crafted of finely worked white lace that must have cost a considerable sum, but which now had mildew creeping at its edges. The woven rug upon the floor was patterned in delicate blues and whites, and atop the dressing table lay a hairbrush, a wooden jewelry box and a scent bottle, not neatly ordered but rather scattered carelessly, as if their owner had left them as she hurried to some engagement, intending to replace them upon her return. Indeed, the whole room had an air of expectancy, as if waiting for its mistress to reappear. The only indication to the contrary was the ominous layer of dust that lay across everything like a mourning veil.

Entranced, I crept farther into the room, leaving the door ajar. Though I perhaps should have felt afraid, oddly I did not. It was as if the benevolent spirit of the former occupant – Lucy Greythorne, I presumed – was watching over the place, and the thought gave me comfort.

I walked over to the dressing table and carefully lifted the lid of the jewelry box. I noticed that the stool before the table was free from dust, and the box itself also seemed to have been wiped clean, as if someone had lately been sitting and looking just as I was. I had expected to find the box empty, but it was not; pinned to a velvet cushion was a brooch in which was encased a golden lock of hair, perhaps from a child. Beside the brooch, on their own cushion, lay two exquisite necklaces – one of diamonds and rubies, one a string of pearls. The box was large, with many drawers, and upon investigation I found it also contained a number of bracelets, rings and beautifully wrought hair ornaments of gold and silver set with precious stones. It seemed odd to keep such valuable trinkets hoarded away in a long-forgotten bedroom, particularly when the Professor had all but confessed he was in financial difficulties, for the jewels would surely be worth a small fortune. Unable to help myself, I selected one of the hair ornaments, of delicate filigreed silver in the shape of a butterfly and set with sapphires, and turned it to better catch the light from the window. I had never owned even paste jewelry, and I was captivated by its beauty.

"*What are you doing?*" I jumped in fright and dropped the hair ornament; it clattered onto the tabletop. The Professor stood in the doorway. His former genial manner had vanished; his eyes were like ice. As he strode into the room I flinched, afraid for one terrible moment he was going to strike me, but he merely snatched up the hair ornament and replaced it in the box.

I scrambled to my feet. "I … I'm sorry, sir – I meant no harm …"

"You have *no right*!" he snarled. "Get out! *Get out!*"

I did not have to be told again; I darted from the room and ran as fast as I could down the hallway, fleeing the wrath in those ice-blue eyes. I had no idea where I was or where I was going, but I didn't care. I was hesitant to return to my chamber or the schoolroom, for I wanted to be as far away from the Professor as possible, at least until he'd had the chance to calm down, and I was afraid he might come looking for me there. Now that the first flush of fear was fading, I could feel my ire rising at the violence of his reaction – for although I had been in the wrong, his behavior had been most ungentlemanly. I would have liked to take him to task on it, but he was my employer and I dared not risk another confrontation.

Eventually I found a small back staircase that led down to the ground floor, and shortly after that I came across a set of tall double doors. Behind them lay the original object of my exploration – the library. I slipped in quietly, shutting the great doors behind me, for I had no wish to be taken unawares again, though even if the Professor discovered me there he could surely have no objection. I leaned against them for a moment, trying to still my racing heart, then raised my head and looked around.

The library was vast, a double-height room which, as far as I could tell, took up one whole wing of the house. Bookshelves spanned every wall; the topmost ones were reached by means of a mezzanine gallery, accessed at strategic points by two wooden spiral staircases. In the middle of the space lay a long reading table, and several comfortable-looking armchairs clustered round a beautifully carved fireplace. A large globe of the world stood off to one side. In the far wall were set enormous picture windows that provided a magnificent view of the island's seaward side. Unlike the drawing room, the library appeared to still be in periodic use; the furniture lay uncovered, and there was little dust to be seen. I wondered if the Professor sometimes came there to study.

Unable to restrain myself in the face of so many books, I climbed one of the spiral staircases to the gallery and began to peruse the shelves. I seemed to have stumbled upon the natural sciences section, though many of the titles were incomprehensible to me. As I continued my search, the books began to evolve into what looked like theology; many of them seemed to concern notions of death and the afterlife and had titles ranging from the scientific to the intrepid, such as *Death: The Last Great Adventure?* Although I was slightly afraid of what I might find inside their covers, nevertheless I found myself drawn to them. I pulled down a volume entitled *Resurrection and Life* and opened it to the first page, but what I read made my spine tingle and I snapped the book shut, feeling as though I had stumbled onto something blasphemous.

I had been raised in Brookvale's strict Methodist tradition, with its emphasis on justice, service and reason and, although my faith had been challenged at times, I still felt it to be strong and robust. I knew where I stood on questions of life, death and resurrection, and I shrank from the thought of mere humans trying to overthrow the natural order of things. I wondered at the Professor's taste in literature, for I should not have liked Sophie to stumble upon such works.

Feeling slightly shaken, I replaced the book and, searching for fiction, returned to the lower level and began examining the shelves there. This was much more promising, and I soon discovered a section containing many well-known works, including those by Mr. Shakespeare, Mr. Dickens and Miss Austen. I selected several and went to sit in one of the great armchairs, anticipating spending the rest of the afternoon in joyful repose. I was soon lost in the depths of *A Midsummer Night's Dream*, my favorite play, with its star-crossed lovers and mystical fairies, remembering how at Brookvale years ago I had played the role of the majestic fairy queen, Titania.

It was only the dimming light that alerted me to the day's passage, and I realized my holiday was all but over. Collecting my other books – *The Pickwick Papers*, *Emma* and *Shakespeare's Sonnets* – I left the library and returned to the schoolroom.

Sophie was asleep in one of the great armchairs, her book fallen to the floor. I shook her shoulder gently. "Wake up, sweetheart. It's almost dinner time."

She stirred and stared at me blearily, as if unsure for a moment who I was.

"You look like Mama," she murmured. I did not know how to reply to this strange pronouncement, so I said nothing.

Jonas entered then, carrying a tray, but it was only set for one.

"The Professor requests you join him for dinner," he said abruptly, setting down the tray and retreating before I could even open my mouth to protest. My heart sank. No doubt after this afternoon's incident the Professor wished to terminate my employment, and perhaps he saw this as a gentler way of breaking the news, though I would have preferred he just come straight out and say it. In truth, I would not be sorry to leave Greythorne Manor and its tragic ghosts, but my heart ached for poor Sophie. It was no life for a bright and vivacious child, stuck here on this miserable island with a father who could barely stand the sight of her.

I watched Sophie eat, then helped her ready herself for bed. That night she requested no story, just rolled over and pulled the covers up to her chin, clutching her doll to her chest. I kissed her and turned down the lamp before retreating to my own room to dress for dinner. I wanted nothing more than to stay in my quarters in blissful solitude, and no doubt many a prisoner had gone to the gallows with a more cheerful countenance than that with which I approached this meal.

Chapter 9

I entered the dining room with my stomach fluttering, unsure of the man I would find within, but he smiled and stood to greet me as he had each time before. There was no trace of the rage I had witnessed that afternoon, yet I found it difficult see him as the charming, congenial host of my first evening; I still remembered how those blue eyes, now so bright and lively, had hardened mercilessly until they were the color of ice. Then again, I reflected, perhaps he had had a right to be angry. I too, no doubt, would have been incandescent with rage had I found a relative stranger trespassing on the quarters of one I had so dearly loved. I swallowed my nervousness, endeavoring to project an image of stately deportment, but under my skirts my knees were trembling.

"Please, Miss Featherstone, sit down," he said, pulling out a chair for me. I sat obediently. "I fear I must beg your pardon," he continued. "I apologize profusely for my behavior toward you this afternoon. I was simply startled to find you in a place where I had expected to see no one."

"It is I who was in the wrong," I said, forcing myself to meet his eyes. "I should not have intruded upon what was so clearly a private place."

"Even so, it does not excuse my reaction," he said as Jonas brought in the first course. "And I wish to make it up to you." He handed me a small cloth-wrapped package that had been sitting before him on the table. I unwrapped it – not without some trepidation – and discovered, to my shock, the exquisite silver and sapphire hair ornament I had so admired this afternoon.

"I ..." I didn't know what to say. "Thank you, sir. I'm sure I don't deserve this."

"Nonsense," he said. "Beautiful jewels were made to adorn beautiful women, and it seems a shame that these should be hidden away. I know it is what Lucy would have wanted. You know, in many ways you remind me of her. Here." He rose and moved behind my chair. Picking up the ornament, he fastened it gently into my hair. His hand lingered on my neck for a moment, his touch soft. I felt myself blushing, and lowered my eyes. But I still needed to be sure

I completely understood the situation. "So … you're not sending me away?"

"Sending you away? Of course not! What a ridiculous notion!" He returned to his seat, placing his napkin across his knees with a flourish. My skin was still tingling where he had touched it.

"I only thought—"

"It was a misunderstanding; it is forgotten, though I would appreciate it if you would in future refrain from wandering outside the bounds of the main living areas. There are parts of this house which are unfortunately falling into disrepair, and they are not completely safe."

I nodded my assent, grateful to have escaped punishment, and flattered by his obvious regard for me. "Tell me, sir," I said, looking to guide the conversation into less-dangerous waters and restore my own equanimity, "what is the Manor's history?" I wondered who had first conceived the idea of building a house in such an inhospitable place, and how they had achieved it, for despite my first impression of the building from across the water, presumably the stone would have had to have been transported from the mainland; there was after all no sign of a quarry on the island. I shivered at the thought of heavily laden barges traversing the narrow channel through the rocks; the first owner must have been mad to attempt such a feat.

The Professor smiled, seemingly pleased by the question. "I don't rightly know," he said. "There have always been stories about the place, as there are about all old houses; you need only ask the villagers. They say the house was built by an eccentric old man nearly two centuries ago; there were some ghastly tales about murdered brides in the cellar, but as far as I know that is merely historical embellishment. I certainly have discovered no such horrors." He laughed, and I smiled with him, noticing how his eyes crinkled pleasantly in merriment. "Even so," he continued, "these stories give a place character. After its original owner died, the house was neglected for a long time. A succession of families bought it – thinking it a romantic spot, perhaps – but only a few of them lived here full-time, and it's said that those who did inevitably encountered some tragedy. There was a little boy who fell down the well, I believe, and another child who perished in a fire in the east wing of the house, though that part has long since been rebuilt. When I bought it, it had once again been suffering a period of neglect – for I believe the previous owner disappeared rather abruptly under controversial circumstances – and I have yet to restore it to my satisfaction. But it provides a secure place for my research, so in that it fulfills its function perfectly."

"Forgive my curiosity, sir, but I would have thought a university to be the natural place of residence for an eminent scientist such as yourself."

A shadow passed over his face, and for a moment I worried I had said something wrong.

"I was based at a university for many years," he said, gazing into the distance as if reliving that time. "But they are not the hotbeds of innovation and learning they purport to be. The students are often stupid and the professors lazy or corrupt. My research was ridiculed, and then, when they finally saw the sense in my ideas, it was nearly taken from me. Jonas was the only one in that nest of vipers whom I was able to trust." He glowered, his black brows lowering like twin thunderclouds.

"Jonas was a student there?" I found it hard to believe such a thing.

The Professor gave a short, barking laugh. "Hardly! He was a man-of-all-work employed around the laboratories. But I soon found him to be circumspect and practical, so I gave him the opportunity to earn a more substantial income and educate himself as my research assistant. He is as loyal as a faithful hound, is Jonas, so when I left the university he chose to come with me. And here we are, some way yet from achieving scientific glory, but not too far off, I trust." He glanced around the room with some satisfaction before his gaze returned to settle on my face. There was a glint in his eye that told me he admired what he found there, and, meeting his gaze, I was surprised at the strength of my own feelings.

"Your research is proceeding well then, sir?"

"It is indeed. You are interested in science, Miss Featherstone?"

"I confess I am, sir, though many do not see it as a respectable diversion for a young lady."

He snorted derisively at this. "It is best remembered that people are fools. I, for instance, would like nothing better than for Sophie to follow in my footsteps, despite her sex."

"That is very progressive of you, sir."

"You and I are of the same mind, I think, Miss Featherstone," he said. "My darling wife sadly had no passion for science, and, like those pathetic university types, could not understand my vision. But you are different, and your interest is fortuitous, for I sometimes find myself wishing for a collaborator. Perhaps one day I shall show you my experiments, when they are a bit closer to fruition."

"Thank you, sir, I should like that."

He smiled, and we ate companionably in silence for some minutes. Then, since he seemed to be in such an amiable mood, I decided to chance my luck. "If you please, sir," I began, "I have another request."

"Of course."

"I was wondering if perhaps Sophie and I might travel to the mainland with Jonas when next he goes."

He considered it only for a moment, and I could see what his answer was to be before he uttered it. There was a subtle change in the air of the room; the pleasant tension that had crackled between us for much of the meal had disappeared, replaced by something less agreeable.

"No, I think not," he said. "Sophie is still young and impressionable, and I do not wish to expose her to the corrupting influences of the village."

"Then perhaps I might go alone?"

"Jonas does not go to Grimly on pleasure-voyages," he said, a harsher note in his voice. "He goes to replenish our supplies, and requires the maximum possible space in which to stow them. So I think it would be best if you remained here and continued your lessons with Sophie." He paused, maybe sensing my disappointment, for he added, "Perhaps next month we might reconsider the situation." But in spite of this late concession, I could tell by his tone that I would not be traveling to Grimly at all in the foreseeable future. I realized, with a clenching in the pit of my stomach, that I was effectively a prisoner at Greythorne Manor, for my liberty depended entirely on the whims of the Professor. But that was ridiculous, of course. He was a handsome, lonely man – albeit with a somewhat quick temper – with whom I seemed to have a lot in common; he was not my jailer.

I shrugged off the uncomfortable thought, and endeavored to comport myself throughout the rest of the meal with passable cheerfulness. When it was over I returned to my room. Stripping off my fine dress to exchange it for one of my plain, everyday gowns, I stood before the mirror in my petticoat, watching the firelight glinting on the silver butterfly as I turned my head. I removed it from my hair and held it in my hands, admiring the intricacy of the work, then I wrapped it in a rag and shoved it to the back of the wardrobe shelf. Despite my efforts to turn my thoughts in a more rational direction, I was no longer sure if it was a token of regard or of possession. The thought was like cold water on the little flame of desire I had been nurturing for the Professor, and I felt my old, sensible self returning.

Shutting the wardrobe door, I dressed in my old, comfortable gown and, settling before the fire, attempted to distract myself from my gloom with the volumes I had brought up from the library.

I was leafing through the first book, *Shakespeare's Sonnets*, when a slip of paper fluttered out from between sonnets seventeen and eighteen. I caught it up and found, to my surprise, a yellowing newspaper clipping. I began to read, feeling a chill creeping down my spine.

30 June 1889

Mrs. Lucy Greythorne, beloved wife of Professor Nathaniel Greythorne, died this morning after suffering a tragic cliff-side fall yesterday. Her husband and young daughter have the sympathy of her many friends in their bereavement. The Father has come down into his garden and has plucked one of the loveliest flowers, in the vigor of youth, and has transplanted it in a higher terrace, where it will bloom with sweeter redolence.

It was almost as if Lucy Greythorne were shadowing my steps today; first I had stumbled upon her bedroom, now her obituary. A cliff-side fall, the clipping said, and heaven knew there were treacherous cliffs enough around the island. In a fit of morbid fascination, I wondered where exactly she had fallen, and whether it had truly been an accident.

Uncomfortable with this line of thought, I slipped the paper back into the book and returned to Shakespeare, only to have a line of poetry catch my eye. Someone had underlined in neat pencil the final couplet of sonnet seventeen: *But were some child of yours alive that time, You should live twice, in it and in my rhyme.*

I could not explain why a simple line of love poetry should unsettle me so, yet it did. I thought of Sophie, and her resemblance to the young woman in the drawing-room portrait; a resemblance that, if my guess were correct, induced in her father an intense and complicated mix of love and aversion. I closed the book and readied myself for bed, seeking to put an end to a strange and unsettling day. I fell asleep to disquieting dreams of gloomy old houses and murdered brides in the cellar.

Chapter 10

In the night I woke, thinking I heard a cry, but when I sat up and listened all was still and quiet. I lay back again, puzzled, telling myself it was just a wild animal or bird, and shortly fell asleep again. In the morning I woke feeling groggy and out of sorts, and would have loved nothing more than to stay in bed. Greythorne Manor's mysteries were beginning to gnaw at my heart, and the dismal grey sky outside, which already held the promise of winter – for October was steadily marching on – did nothing to lift my spirits.

Sophie, when I woke her, was similarly depressed; her face was paler than usual, and dark circles ringed her eyes. She looked exhausted and ill enough to worry me.

"Did you have nightmares again?" I asked as I helped her dress. Perhaps I had heard a cry after all. She shook her head, but didn't say a word.

She ate enough breakfast to satisfy me of her health, but remained listless and uninterested throughout our morning lessons. Rather than forcing her outside on such a miserable day – for the lowering clouds had already delivered one drenching during the morning and were threatening another – I lit the schoolroom fire and we sat in front of it in silence. I was in the rocking chair as usual, darning a pair of Sophie's stockings, while my charge lay before the hearth, a book in front of her. By and by, however, she rose and came to where I sat, misery written across her face.

"Why, Sophie, what's wrong?" I asked. She did not respond, but crawled into my lap, laid her head against my shoulder and began to weep. Confused and not a little distressed, I held her tightly and said nothing, just rocked her back and forth.

After a while the storm of tears blew itself out; she remained curled on my knee, and I held her until she dozed off. Something very strange was going on. I stared into the flames, but could not even begin to puzzle it out.

When Sophie woke she seemed more like her old self, though still prone to waves of melancholy. After a simple dinner I put her to bed early and sang to her until she slept, before going downstairs to dine with the Professor, though I would much rather have stayed in the schoolroom – I was still feeling unsettled from our encounter the previous evening.

He, too, looked tired and worn, as if he'd had many late nights or suffered some crushing disappointment. Although reluctant to burden him when he was clearly in such low spirits himself, I felt I nevertheless had a duty to inform him of his daughter's condition.

"I'm sorry to trouble you, sir," I began, "but I wished to talk to you about Sophie."

"She is misbehaving?"

"Oh no, nothing like that. But she is not herself; she complains often of nightmares and seems tired and listless."

He simply shrugged, seemingly unconcerned. "All children have nightmares now and then, Miss Featherstone," he said. "I should have thought a governess, of all people, would have known that."

I bridled, but forced myself to take a deep breath. "That is true, sir, but rarely with such violence or regularity. I thought a brief change of scene might help restore her spirits, and was wondering if you had reconsidered my request about a day on the mainland?"

His gaze hardened, and I realized too late that I had overstepped the mark. "I thought I made my position more than clear during our last discussion," he said. "It is not practical for either you or Sophie to travel to the mainland at this time; Jonas is simply too busy. I would have thought this was a small matter for a woman of your intelligence to understand, and I wish to hear no more of it."

I bowed my head so he could not read my thoughts in my eyes. "Yes, sir."

The rest of the meal was strained, and I believe we both wished it over long before its end. As soon as I could I returned to the schoolroom, feeling deeply unsettled. It could be – perhaps was even likely – that the Professor's excuses were not in fact excuses at all, but the plain truth. Perhaps I *would* get my chance to visit the village in time, when Jonas was less burdened.

All of this sounded reasonable, and yet there was something in my heart that told me it was not so. The Professor had revealed little in his speech, but there had been something about his countenance, some little flickering of the eyes perhaps, that had given the lie to his words. The revelation of a harsher side to his character had taken me by surprise, and I was glad I had not allowed my early infatuation to run away with me. But what possible reason could he have for keeping me on the island? I was surely being ridiculous, an overreaction brought on by an acute awareness of my own vulnerability. Because of course, if the Professor *was* keeping me there on purpose, I had no one to whom I could write for help. I had no powerful connections, no one to be perturbed by my silence and come looking for me. Even Matron did not expect regular letters from me, and so would not notice their absence.

On retiring to bed I deliberately left open the two doors between my quarters and Sophie's, so as to hear anything unusual that may occur in the night, but my rest was sound and undisturbed. The next day Sophie's temper seemed much improved, and we settled back into our old routine, the only difference being that I now left the doors open every night. Sophie's learning was progressing remarkably, and there were still enough days of sunshine and relative warmth to enable us to spend a fair portion of our time outside roaming the island. To my mind, however, the most fertile ground for exploration remained the house itself. I was convinced the key to Greythorne's mysteries lay somewhere deep in the bowels of the old stone manor, but it was off-limits to me, at least for now. I could not risk the Professor's ire by being discovered again in areas I should not be. His temper was so unpredictable – there was no telling what he might do.

And so the days and weeks crept on, with each night growing a little longer than the one before. I began to despair of ever leaving this desolate piece of rock, which was becoming even less hospitable as winter drew nearer. I looked forward with no joy to the stormy, freezing maelstrom of the cold months, when the seas would rise high, and doubtless even Greythorne Manor's thick stone walls would be unable to keep the wind at bay.

The season was previewed on All Hallow's Eve, a few weeks after Sophie's mysterious attack of emotional infirmity. A violent storm had come up, and between the crashing of the thunder and the pounding of the waves against the island's rocky shore the din was fit to wake the dead. Sophie and I supped together in the schoolroom; the Professor had not summoned me to join him, and I was glad, for Sophie was quite discomfited by the storm. I initially wondered why this should be, given that she'd spent her whole life on this rocky little island and had no doubt witnessed many such tempests, but as I tucked her into bed she whispered the answer to me: "The dead walk tonight."

"Nonsense," I said brusquely, for I did not believe in ghosts, and given the setting and the wild weather I was determined that her imagination should not run away with her.

"It's true. I've seen them."

"Come now, Sophie, go to sleep. There's nothing here that will hurt you."

She said nothing, but her dark eyes were accusatory, as if I did not know what I was talking about. It was a look old beyond her years, and I suddenly felt myself a shame-faced liar, for were there not perhaps plenty of things there that would hurt her, only hominal rather than spectral? At length, however, sleep she did, and I retired shortly after, for the wind was fierce and even the schoolroom fire could not adequately combat its chill.

I soon slept, but was woken deep in the night by the sound of crying and a thump. At first I thought it was the wind, which was still howling fiercely, but after some minutes I decided to investigate. The crying had grown more distant now, as if whatever it was was moving away from me. I climbed out of bed and pulled on my dressing gown and slippers, lighting the candle end that sat beside my bed. Creeping quietly, lest I should be heard, I ventured into the schoolroom, but all was as I had left it when I went to bed. Shaking my head at my ridiculous fears, I decided to check on Sophie before returning to my room. Shielding the candle with my hand – for I did not want the light to wake her – I tiptoed into her chamber. The bed shone white in a ray of moonlight that slanted between the curtains. The covers had been thrown back, and Sophie was nowhere to be seen.

I reeled in horror, almost dropping the candle, and I confess my first irrational thought was that she had indeed been snatched from her bed by some ghost. But that was ridiculous, and as I forced my emotions under control I began to look at the situation more clearly. Perhaps she was sleep-walking? But I had never known her to do such a thing before. I opened the bedroom door and peered out into the long gallery, but there was no sign of her. Part of me wanted to rush off immediately in search of her, but I knew it would be hopeless to go dashing all over the house in the middle of the night given the Manor's twisty passages and steep staircases. I had only my stub of candle, which was rapidly burning low, and I did not have another close at hand. Reluctantly, and almost sick with worry, I returned to the schoolroom, wrapped myself in a blanket from my bed – for the fire had long since died down – and sat in the rocking-chair, resolving to stay there until Sophie returned.

I was woken many hours later by the grey dawn light drifting in through the unshuttered schoolroom windows. I blinked, disoriented, unsure of quite where I was or how I had come to be there. Gradually I became conscious of a stiffness in my neck from sleeping in the chair, and then it all came back to me. I threw off my blanket and hastened to Sophie's room.

Sophie was back in her bed, sleeping as soundly as if she had never left it; the only thing slightly out of place was the bedroom door, which was ajar the tiniest crack. I shook my head to clear it, wondering if I had been dreaming. Not wanting to wake her, I contented myself with peering closely at her. She appeared unharmed, and her breathing was deep and regular. I backed quietly out of the room and returned to my own bed, for it was still early, but I could not sleep. There was something odd about this business, and I vowed I would not rest until I got to the bottom of it.

I must have dozed again, for it was full sunlight when I woke, and far past the usual hour of my rising. I washed and dressed hastily, trying to rub the bleary sleep from my eyes. In the schoolroom I found Sophie already dressed and tucking into breakfast. She was eating heartily, although her eyes were once again sunken and shadowed with fatigue. I appraised her critically, wondering if she'd lost weight, which she could ill afford.

"Good morning, Sophie."

She raised her eyes and smiled at me, her mouth full of toast. I sat down at the table and helped myself to some porridge.

"Did you sleep well?" I asked, wishing to see if she would confess to late-night wanderings.

She shrugged. "I had another nightmare."

This puzzled me exceedingly. In the dormitory at Brookvale many of the younger girls had suffered from nightmares, and the whole room had been roused by their cries. Yet I had heard nothing from Sophie, and she had certainly not come running to me for comfort, as children are wont to do in such circumstances. Perhaps she was simply a silent sufferer; but how then to explain the midnight absence from her bed?

"Tell me, Sophie, do you sleep-walk?" Even as I asked the question I wondered whether the sleep-walker ever knew that he did so. It was thus unsurprising that she shook her head. "Can you tell me about your nightmare?"

She shrugged, staring down at her plate. "It was the same one as always. I was lying on a table in Papa's laboratory, and a man in a mask was bending over me with a needle in his hand. I screamed but no one could hear me and then I couldn't move my arms and legs, and that's all I remember. It's always the same – I wake up after that."

This confounded me, though a little germ of an idea had already begun to sprout. But it was too horrifying for me to contemplate further, so I buried it deep and attempted to find a more rational explanation for the situation. I let the subject drop, as Sophie was clearly distressed by the memory of her dream. "Shall we go for a walk today after lessons?" I asked. "It seems a shame to waste such a beautiful morning." The blustery gale of the previous night had blown itself out, leaving the sky a calm, clean-washed blue. It would still be cold outside, I knew, but any respite from the vicious wind was very welcome.

Consequently, on completing our morning lessons we ate our luncheon in the schoolroom then ventured outside. The island had clothed herself in her best raiment for us; the sun shone brightly, setting the pine trees around the house a glowing emerald hue, and even the dull grey rocks seemed brightened. A breeze still blew – inevitable when by the sea – but it was gentle, of a kind calculated to quicken the blood and strengthen the appetite, rather than the ferocious squalls of recent weeks.

We meandered along our usual route around the perimeter of the island, and as always I let Sophie run ahead of me. It was good for the child to get some exercise, particularly when she'd been looking so sallow and tired, and I also took delight in her curiosity and fascination with the natural world. Every so often she would come dashing back, wanting to show me some pretty shell or odd-shaped rock she'd discovered. I smiled and joined in the games, exclaiming at her treasures. I was growing unaccountably fond of this wild little girl and her ways, which, though odd, were somehow enchanting.

In the course of our wanderings we happened across a sheer cliff that dropped away steeply to a little beach; the same beach, I realized belatedly, where Jonas kept the boat. We had been past there many times before, but had rarely paused, for it was unremarkable save providing the only safe egress from the island. Today, however, Sophie halted and walked out along the cliff-top.

"Sophie, be careful," I called, hastening to join her. "How could I face your father if you took a fall?"

She turned and looked at me then, and my heart leaped within my chest, for it was the cold, discerning gaze of a much older woman. "He wouldn't care," she said.

"Sophie!"

"It's true. This is where my mother died, and I know he wishes it had been me instead."

I was dumbstruck and could only gaze at her in horror, for such pronouncements were chilling from anyone, let alone a child. I watched Sophie as she looked on the spot with the gaze of the familiar, and came to a realization.

"Were you here the night she died?"

She nodded, not meeting my eyes. She must have been very young, I thought, no more than three years old, but great trauma has a way of imprinting itself upon the mind, even that of a little child.

"I don't remember much," she said. "We were running. She was carrying me. Someone cried out. Then we fell. It's all a blur." All this was said bloodlessly, as if she had replayed the scene many times in her mind until it had lost its emotional grip on her. But hearing it for the first time sent shivers down my spine.

"Come on, sweetheart," I said, disquiet making me brusque. "Let's return to the house. I wish to hear you play your new piece this afternoon." Anything to quit this troubled, unhealthy spot.

The rest of the afternoon passed swiftly and uneventfully; Sophie seemed unaffected by her earlier revelations, though they continued to trouble me. We ate our dinner early, and I was glad I did not have to face the Professor that night. Later, Sophie read by the fire while I sewed, until she almost fell asleep lying on the hearth. I put her to bed then retired myself, for the night was growing chill. Lying in bed, I pondered the events of the day. The wind had picked up again after sunset, and as I lay there listening to it wuthering round the house like a distressed soul I thought of Lucy Greythorne, who could not have been so very much older than I was now. In my half-doze I saw her, a young mother clutching her child, running headlong through the blustery night – but why? What had so terrified her that she had chosen to make such a desperate dash for freedom rather than face it? Then, to be caught so cruelly at the final pass; it made me shudder. Did her spirit even now haunt these walls, striving still to protect her daughter? The thought was rather profane, but if ever there was a place destined to be haunted by the unquiet dead it was Greythorne Manor.

Chapter 11

For the past few months I had dined with the Professor at least once a week, but as November unfolded I began to see less and less of him. He must have been working hard, for when I did glimpse his countenance I noticed how thin and worn he looked – quite different from the handsome, charming man I had met upon my arrival.

One day in mid-November Sophie and I were sitting at the schoolroom table, poring over history books, when we were interrupted by the opening door. I knew at once who it must be, for Jonas always knocked, and, sure enough, the Professor entered. I was shocked by his appearance, for even though I had previously thought him much altered, I was ill prepared for how unwell he looked. His face was thin, almost gaunt; the sunken cheeks made his pale eyes seem preternaturally large. His moustache was still luxuriant, but looked in need of a trim. He also appeared to have lost a considerable amount of weight; his trousers, shirt and waistcoat all drooped on his thin frame as if they had been intended for a much larger man. I suspected he had been sleeping little, for he seemed much fatigued, and though I knew from my irregular meals with him that his appetite was unaltered, I guessed he was of the temperament to become so absorbed in his work as to forget at other times to take sustenance.

All these calculations I made in the blink of an eye, and hoped I did so without his notice. It was unusual for him to enter the schoolroom; indeed, entire weeks passed without us seeing hide or hair of him. I wondered that he could bear to be parted so long from his daughter, but it did not seem to concern him. For her part, Sophie had never remarked on his absence in my hearing, but I surmised that this was the result of expectations dampened by long periods of desolation, rather than by a want of feeling.

"Hello, Papa," Sophie said.

"Sophie; Miss Featherstone." He offered me a small half-bow, glancing at his daughter with something that on a different face might have been a smile. "I've come to advise you that I shall be rowing over to the mainland today, and expect to be gone several weeks. There are some materials that I must locate for my latest experiment. Jonas will remain here and will see to your needs."

Sophie had jumped to her feet at hearing 'mainland'; now she ran to her father and tugged at his coat. "May I come, Papa? *Please*?" Her cheeks glowed with sudden excitement; with her bright eyes imploring him she was the very picture of youthful supplication.

The Professor, however, was unmoved by these childish pleas, though he did pat her head in a somewhat affectionate manner. "No, my dear," he said in a tone I recognized as final, "this is a business matter. It's no place for little children. You stay here with Miss Featherstone and learn your lessons, there's a good girl." Sophie stuck her bottom lip out as if about to protest, but I gave her a warning glance and she thought better of it, returning to her seat in silence.

"Very well," he said. "I must away; my business awaits. Look for me in a month or six weeks. Be good, Sophie, and mind Miss Featherstone."

"Yes, Papa."

"Farewell, sir."

"Well, Sophie," I said as the door closed behind him, "it looks like it's just you and me for a while."

"And Jonas."

"Yes, of course – and Jonas."

*

It would have been reasonable to expect the Professor's absence to leave a hole in the household, but in fact things went on much as they always had; we saw so little of him even when he was here that it was now possible much of the time to forget he was gone. The lack of his mercurial temper, however, did have a relaxing effect upon those who remained; Sophie seemed to be sleeping better and no longer complained of nightmares, and even Jonas's countenance appeared slightly softened. And although I occasionally missed the Professor's sharp wit and engaging conversation – for there were times when I longed for sophisticated adult discourse, which Jonas was in no position to provide – I was happier knowing I could wander the house and grounds at will without fear of stumbling upon something I shouldn't and bringing his wrath down upon my unfortunate head.

Accordingly, I took again to exploring the house when I could, but found little to interest me save myriad disused rooms, their contents covered in dust sheets. I did not return to Lucy's chamber, for I felt I must respect the Professor's wishes, and in any case I found it terribly sad. Sophie dragged me once more through the secret passage, though I insisted we take a candle this time, and I was far less terrified than before.

We likewise continued our explorations of the island, though it was so small there was really very little to discover. But the flora, insects and bird life provided much material for our natural history studies, and I also encouraged Sophie to write down the fanciful stories she told me about the sea-pixies who inhabited this or that cove, or the seal-woman who could sometimes be glimpsed basking on the rocks on moonlit nights. They were strange, beautiful stories for a young girl to dream up, but Sophie was not an average child, and I delighted in hearing them. I had the feeling she would be a great woman of letters one day, if she could ever get off this God-forsaken rock.

It was during one of our walks, round a part of the island off our usual route, that we happened across a large boulder set on the cliff-top. Sophie had been prattling on as normal, but upon seeing the rock she quieted, and I wondered if she were dreaming up some tale of its origin. It certainly struck me as odd, perched there on the cliff like a standing stone of legend, and I walked over to examine it.

"What's this, Sophie?" I asked, but my charge had not followed me, running instead further along the path. I let her go and paused for a moment, then walked around the strange edifice. It was only when I saw the seaward side that I understood Sophie's reticence, for carved into the stone was the name *Lucy Greythorne*, and her dates of birth and death. As I had guessed, she had been very young: only twenty-five years old at her passing. At first I thought it simply a memorial stone, but then I remembered

Mrs. Greenslade's words, all those months ago: "He wouldn't even allow poor Lucy a decent burial in the graveyard here, though she were Grimly born and bred – he took her back to that island of his. If there was ever a place to keep a body from eternal rest that would be it, but he couldn't be prevailed upon ..."

"Sophie," I asked as I caught up to her, "is that your mother's grave?" She nodded, but as she clearly did not wish to discuss it further, I let the matter drop.

We returned shortly thereafter to the house, for the wind had picked up, and ominous clouds were rolling in, chased by the distant rumble of thunder. By the time Jonas brought our dinner the wind was howling round the house and a heavy rain had begun to fall.

"Happen it's going to be a nasty one tonight," Jonas said as he set down the tray. I believed him, not least because very little shook the taciturn manservant out of his reserve, so there must indeed be a bad storm coming if he felt the need to mention it.

The wind grew stronger, draughts of it finding their way like cold fingers into the room, no matter how many cracks we stopped up around doors and windows. It even gusted fitfully down the chimney, causing the fire to smoke and billow. Eventually both Sophie and I tired of it and retired to bed.

I was woken in the night by a clap of thunder so loud I almost expected it to come crashing through the ceiling. Sitting up, I groped for a candle, thinking

I ought to check on Sophie, but there was no need; at that instant a little white figure came dashing in and flung itself at me. I held her tightly as the wind howled round the house, the thunder and lightning warring across the skies. Eventually the worst of the storm passed, though the rain continued to pound, and we both fell asleep with it drumming in our ears.

I woke some hours later to a wan grey dawn trickling in between the curtains. I lay there listening for the wind, but all was quiet; the tempest had blown itself out. Sophie was still asleep, curled up on the other side of the bed like a little rag doll, her fair hair spread across the pillow. I left her sleeping and rose to wash and dress, wondering if there had been any damage done to the house in the night.

When Jonas brought the breakfast I asked him, but he just shrugged. "A few trees've come down round the island," he said, "but this old house has withstood worse'n that. Later I'll go and see how things stand."

Sophie was awake by this time, and as she sat down to breakfast she was unable to stop talking about the storm, with the excited air of one who has faced utter destruction and survived. With each telling of the tale the storm got worse and her own bravery increased, until I decided to put a stop to this exercise in exaggeration by suggesting we go for a walk and survey the damage. This proposal was met, as I had expected, with resounding enthusiasm.

The damage, it turned out, was quite severe. The house was still standing and seemed to have fared remarkably well, for as Jonas said, it had withstood far worse in its time. But his characterization of a couple of trees come down around the island was a gross underestimation. A number of the big old pines had cracked and split, and several had fallen; one or two even looked as if they had been struck by lightning. The fierce rain had washed away entire heaps of earth, leaving gaping holes around the rocks. The storm had given the island a completely new character.

It was not until we wandered up to Lucy Greythorne's grave, however, that I received my biggest shock. Sophie had once again dashed ahead, but I made for the gravesite, wanting, I think, to check that the poor woman's rest had not once again been disturbed. What I found jolted me to my core. The earth around the stone had all but washed away, leaving a gaping crater. Gingerly I peered down, expecting to see a coffin or, God forbid, the remains of Lucy herself, but there was nothing. I crouched beside the hole; it was certainly deep enough to unearth even the most decent of interments, and I imagined she could not have been buried too deeply, for digging through the rocky soil would have been painfully difficult. I looked around, even peering over the cliff, but there was no sign of any remains. Unnerved, I was for once actually relieved to see Jonas farther down the hill, making his way back to the house. I ran as fast as I could over the uneven ground, taking care not to twist my ankle on some loose stone, and caught him as he stopped to inspect the damage to the pines. He listened to my garbled tale with some confusion, his eyebrows rising.

"Don't worry, miss," he said with uncharacteristic gentleness. "The mistress ain't there."

"But that's what I'm *telling* you, Jonas! She's been washed away!" I was becoming exasperated by his inability – or unwillingness – to understand.

"No, she hasn't, miss," he said calmly. "Listen to me: *She ain't there.*"

Finally I realized what he meant, though the reply raised more questions than it answered. "You mean that's not her grave up there on the cliff? Is she interred elsewhere?" But Jonas's eyes had become hooded, and I could see he was not going to answer my questions. As I was about to probe further, Sophie came dashing up, full of chatter about the things she'd seen and the damage to the pine trees, and the moment was lost.

Our lessons were something of a failure that day; Sophie was still too excited about the storm to settle down and study properly, and I was preoccupied with Jonas's words. Eventually I gave up and let Sophie go and play with her dolls, while I sat by the fire, pretending to read but actually pondering the mystery

of Lucy Greythorne. For if her grave was not with
its memorial stone on the cliff, then where was it?
Perhaps the poor woman really was doomed to walk
the island for eternity. But that was ridiculous, and I
shook my head in exasperation at my own thoughts.
She had to be lying somewhere, and I couldn't help
feeling that, on discovering where, I would find the
answers I sought.

Chapter 12

Jonas was kept busy over the following days cleaning up after the storm, and I did not have the opportunity to question him again. Indeed, after our conversation I suspected he was deliberately avoiding me; I had evidently touched some sort of nerve, or perhaps he had revealed more than he should have and was now regretting it. Whatever the reason, it was clear I was unlikely to obtain further information from that source.

As winter closed in I began to feel more and more oppressed by my surroundings. The days were getting far shorter now; darkness came with the late afternoon, and the sun was not showing its face until after eight in the morning. I knew that before long the mainland fells would have their first snowfalls. I wondered if it would snow on the island, though

I doubted it. But the seas were bound to get stormier – would the island be cut off from the mainland? The channel was short, but it was relatively shallow and consequently quite choppy even at the best of times. Did Jonas have enough supplies laid up to last us through the winter? These thoughts circled and descended like carrion-birds, and once they took roost I had difficulty dislodging them. I had known I would not be leaving Greythorne Manor for some time, but the thought of being physically unable to do so even in the Professor's absence was profoundly disquieting. I could not now tell if his violent and mercurial temper or the rocks and waves surrounding his strange little fiefdom frightened me more.

During the day I attempted to put such thoughts from my mind, for Sophie's sake if not my own sanity. She seemed undisturbed by the worsening weather, but then I supposed growing up in such a place made one immune to its idiosyncrasies. No doubt she would have been disquieted by the constant bustle and noise of the city. For her, life was an endless cycle of schoolwork and play, and I congratulated myself that she seemed to be thriving on it. Now that her sleep was less disturbed she was beginning to look healthier; the sallowness had left her cheeks and the shadows were fading from beneath her eyes.

As Sophie's health improved, however, my own declined. My dreams became populated by a host of ghoulish horrors, though I dreamed most of Lucy Greythorne. Ever since Sophie had told me how she had died, the scene had haunted me, and I relived it in my nightmares – sometimes as Sophie, watching her mother fall to her death, and sometimes, worse still, as Lucy herself. I always woke just as I tumbled over the cliff, and would find myself drenched in sweat and tangled in my bedsheets.

A week or so after the big storm, Jonas made an unexpected announcement when he brought our evening meal.

"I'm going to the mainland tomorrow to get supplies before winter sets in." It was a plain statement in his usual gruff tone, but to me it was a golden opportunity. I jumped up, and had to stop myself clutching at his sleeve.

"Take us with you, Jonas," I implored, remembering how not so very long ago Sophie had begged the same thing of the Professor. "Please. We won't get another chance for months."

I had expected him to dismiss me out of hand, but he – I could hardly countenance it – smiled. He had never looked at me properly until that moment, but I could see... was it affection? At any rate, there was something new in his eyes.

"And what would you do on the mainland?"

I already had an answer to this. "I'll take Sophie to see Frances Greenslade at the Grimly Arms," I said.

"She's a good woman and I'd dearly love to visit her. We'll have luncheon there and then return with you in the afternoon. It's all perfectly harmless."

Jonas ruminated for a moment, and I crossed my fingers.

"Professor won't like it," he muttered.

"Well," I said, seeing my chance slipping away, "we won't tell him if you won't." I knew I was setting a terrible example, encouraging Sophie to lie to her father, but I was becoming desperate. I very much wanted to see Frances and to once again engage in adult conversation. The thought of many more months here in this vast isolation was almost enough to make me weep.

Some of my feelings must have showed on my face, for Jonas looked at me shrewdly.

"Young ladies need female company," he mumbled to himself. "Mistress was the same, but the Professor never understood."

I nodded hopefully, seeing he was relenting.

"Very well," he said, his old gruffness returning. "We'll leave at nine o'clock tomorrow morning to catch the tide. Mind you're ready." Then he turned and left without another word, closing the door behind him.

Sophie was almost bouncing in her chair with excitement, and it was all I could do to make her hush. "Come now," I said, "eat your supper, there's a good girl. And then it's off to bed with you – it's a big day tomorrow." She acquiesced, occasionally sneaking a cheeky grin up at me. I was afraid she would be too het-up to sleep, but I need not have feared; she was asleep almost as soon as her head touched the pillow. I retired to my own bed shortly afterwards, my stomach fluttering with anticipation.

*

I woke early and was unable to return to sleep, so I rose and pottered around in the half-light until it was time to rouse Sophie. Mornings did not usually agree with her, but although at first she was groggy and reticent as usual, as soon as she remembered what was to come she bounced out of bed. Going to the mainland was of course even more of a treat for her than it was for me.

I helped her dress in one of her nicer gowns – for it would not do to pay calls in house-clothes – and we ate the breakfast Jonas provided, though my stomach was so restless I wondered if I should be able to keep anything down. I had no reason to be nervous other than the unpredictability of the sea voyage, but perhaps it was my conscience twinging with the knowledge we were acting against the Professor's wishes. Such thoughts were ridiculous, I chided myself; after all, the Professor would surely not begrudge me a visit to a friend. Again the thought arose: he was not trying to keep me prisoner – was he?

When breakfast was over I found thick woolen shawls for Sophie and myself – for it was sure to be cold on the water – then, warmly wrapped, we set off for the boat. It felt strange to be going down the cliff path in the knowledge that for the first time in several months I could actually leave the island. I was exhilarated, but there was a hint of sadness too, even though I would be returning that night. I wondered how it was that the big old house with its drafty passageways and odd occupants should exert such a sway over me.

Jonas was already at the boat waiting for us, his toe tapping impatiently. The bow was full of sacks – presumably in which to bring home the provisions – and as soon as he had helped us into the stern he pushed off and began to row. Much as I had on my first voyage, I watched again with interest as he navigated the crashing waves around the rocks. The sea was wilder now than it had been in the summertime, tossing the boat to and fro like a cork, but though we were splashed with spray I thankfully felt no seasickness. I glanced surreptitiously at Sophie, worried she might be ill, but she was watching the water intently with a grin stretching from ear to ear. She was enjoying herself immensely.

Once we were free of the rocks the sea began to settle and the trip became more pleasant. The day was shaping up to be calm and fine – the first such we'd had for some time – and Grimly's little white houses were bathed in golden light, giving the village a warm, ethereal appearance. Shutting my eyes for a moment, I basked in the sunlight, feeling as if an enormous weight had been lifted from my shoulders. I glanced back towards the island, where the house crouched on its rocky outcrop like a hibernating beast. I did not hate it – in fact, there was something about its wildness that stirred the depths of my soul – but it was a presence that weighed on the mind like an old regret. It was full of lost dreams and shattered hopes, and I was glad to leave it, if only for the day. I wondered if Lucy had felt this way too, and if she had ever had a chance to escape.

We pulled into the quay, to the same mooring-place as all those months earlier. Jonas tossed the sacks out onto the wharf, then hopped out – very nimbly for a man of his age – and offered his hand first to me and then to Sophie. It took a few moments for me to find my shore-legs, and the quay seemed to bob under me, but Sophie suffered no such affliction. She took my hand and practically dragged me up the street, after I promised Jonas to return at two o'clock.

It was still quite early, for the voyage in its entirety had taken only about half an hour. I wondered whether the day was advanced enough for us to call on the Greenslades, but when we got to the inn we found its door flung wide in welcome, and I remembered that Frances often provided breakfast for the fishermen returning from their night on the water.

The interior of the inn was just as I remembered – cozy and smelling of furniture polish – with a bright fire burning in the grate. There was no one to be seen, so Sophie and I seated ourselves before the cheerful blaze. The warmth made Sophie drowsy; she leaned her head against my shoulder, yawning.

"Well now, here's a sight for sore eyes!" Frances Greenslade came bustling in, carrying a tray of glasses. She deposited them on the bar and hurried over to us. I nudged Sophie awake and clambered to my feet. "How are you, Nell? And this can't be little Sophie!" She clasped my hands warmly, kissing me on both cheeks. Sophie gave her prettiest smile.

"I've been keeping a look-out for you all these months," Frances said, sitting down with us before the fire, "but I'd almost given up hope, what with winter nearly come and all. Jenny Ward swore she saw the Professor at the train station a few weeks back, but she couldn't remember if you were with him or not. Has he returned?"

I shook my head. "He doesn't know we're here." I felt I could trust Frances, and was enthused by her warm welcome.

She gave me a knowing look. "Well, he won't hear it from me, love. And now, how about some breakfast?"

We gratefully accepted her offer – for our own morning meal had been meager, on account of having to make the boat on time – and we were soon tucking into plates of eggs and home-cured bacon. The Grimly Arms served hearty farmers' fare, and Sophie was clearly relishing the novelty of it.

"Now then, Sophie," Frances said when we were finished, "what do you say to a special treat? If you go out to the yard you'll find there's a litter of new puppies in one of the stables – they're only a few weeks old." Sophie sprang up in delight, her face more animated than I had ever seen her, and followed Frances along the hallway, while I returned to the fire.

"She's utterly smitten," Frances said, returning and lowering herself into one of the homely armchairs. "She'll be amused for hours. Now, tell me, how are you finding life at the Manor?"

I almost didn't know where to start. "Have you ever been there?" I asked, for it would be difficult to describe the place to one who had never seen it.

"No, never. The Professor isn't overly fond of visitors, as I'm sure you're well aware."

"Well, it's a queer old place ..." I began. I told her about the house – though not the secret passage – and the way the wind wuthered, and the salty smell of the air. Then we got to talking about the big storm, and

I remembered the odd conversation with Jonas about Lucy's grave.

"Tell me, Frances, did you know Lucy Greythorne?"

"Oh aye, I should think I did. Lucy and her sister Isabella were great friends with my Bess. The three of them and Katie Drabble from Lark Hill Farm were thick as thieves. Good girls, all of them. And now Bess and Katie and Isabella are all married with little ones of their own, and poor Lucy has gone to be with God." She sighed. "And she was always the one who showed such promise, though I mean no insult to the others. My Bess is a strong, reliable girl, and the other two are the same, but none of them could hold a candle to Lucy. She was extremely bright; she could run rings round them all. I suspect little Sophie's the same?"

I nodded. Sophie was still young, but her intelligence was already formidable.

"If she'd been a lad she would have been off to university, no question," Frances continued. "Her people would have found the money somehow. But as a girl ... Well, marriage was her best hope. And the tragedy of it is that I think she knew it. She became a professor's wife, when really she longed to *be* the professor." She sighed again. "But that is the way of the world, is it not? And I don't think she was unhappy to be marrying Nathaniel. At her wedding she was as joyous and glowing as any bride I've ever seen." She smiled ruefully, staring into the fire in reminiscence. A piece of wood slipped, sending glittering sparks shooting up the chimney.

"But there, I'm prattling on. I haven't mentioned any of this for years; you might have noticed people in the village don't like to talk about the Professor or the Manor." She laughed. "Though they'll quite happily discuss everything else."

I nodded; I remembered well the reticence I had encountered the last time I was in Grimly. "Why won't people talk about it?" I asked. "It's just an isolated old house – nothing so very dreadful."

Frances shrugged. "I don't know," she said. "The Manor was abandoned for many years, and when the Professor came, people in the village hoped he would give the old place a new lease of life. But then there was the terrible business with poor Lucy."

"I found a newspaper clipping about her death," I said, for I was confident Frances would not reveal my snooping to the Professor. "It said she died in a fall." I did not tell her that Sophie had also talked to me of her mother's tragic end.

"Aye, right enough," Frances said. "Though what she was doing running along the cliff in the middle of the night is anyone's guess."

"Perhaps something had frightened her."

"Perhaps. The poor lass was terribly unhappy towards the end. You know, she used to write to me sometimes."

"Really?"

"Aye. Jonas would bring the letters when he came over to fetch supplies. It was all very hush-hush, for I believe the Professor disliked her communicating with people in the village – even with her family. But Jonas would often come in here for a pint before rowing back to the island, and he would slip the letters to me with his money. They were usually disguised as grocery lists, which I think was how she got them past the Professor. Sometimes she'd ask me to tell her news to her family, but more often than not she requested me not to reveal the letters' contents, for I think she was afraid of worrying her parents and sister. She was a stoic, independent sort, and she knew her marriage had helped her parents, so she was loath to burden them."

"The poor girl," I said, thinking of the pretty, smiling face in the portrait.

"I think she was happy enough to begin with," Frances said. "It perhaps wasn't the life she would have chosen for herself, but she was determined to make the best of it." She sighed. "But the Manor was also very different back then. There was a near-full complement of servants, most of whom came from the village – the butler, Reynolds; the housekeeper, Mrs. Andrews; and the cook, Mrs. Johnston, were all local. Then there were two housemaids, Anna and Jennifer I think their names were, and two footmen, who were all from round these parts originally before they went into service. And of course there was Jonas."

"What do you know about Jonas?" I asked, for I remained as curious as ever about the enigmatic man-of-all-work, and Frances seemed keen to unburden herself. She had bottled up all her thoughts and memories of Lucy and Greythorne Manor for so long that it was like opening a floodgate.

"Not much at all, really," she said. "He's never been one for talking, has Jonas. But I understand he was some sort of laboratory assistant or similar at the university, and when the Professor left he came too, though goodness knows why you'd choose to leave the hallowed halls of learning for a place like Greythorne Manor." She laughed, though there was a hollow ring to it. "But then maybe he didn't have a choice. I can't imagine there were many willing to employ him, for neither his countenance nor his temperament endear him. I've always found him to be an upright sort of character, but although I've been acquainted with him for many years I can't in good conscience say I really know him at all."

The grandfather clock in the corner chimed suddenly, making us both jump. "Eh, now, is that the time?" Frances said. "Arthur'll be in soon wanting a cup of tea. Will you have one?"

"Thank you, yes," I said. "I'll just go and check on Sophie." I went out the back passageway, through the large kitchen to the cobbled yard. The place was lively with industrious noise, and the smell of horses and produce rose up to greet me. Mr. Greenslade was there, talking to a supplier, while two yard-men unloaded crates from the back of a dray. He stopped when he saw me and raised his hand in greeting.

"The little lass is over there," he called, pointing to one of the stables. I thanked him and crossed the yard. The top part of the half-door was open, the bottom half closed, so I leaned my elbows on it and peered into the stall.

Sophie was sitting in the straw, surrounded by eight brindled puppies. Their mother lay over to the side but seemed untroubled by the interloper.

"Aren't they wonderful?" Sophie said when she saw me watching. "Oh, how I wish we could keep one!"

I could see where this sentiment was heading, and quickly disabused her of the notion. "Come now," I said, holding out my hand. "Come and have tea with me and Mrs. Greenslade." She rose and slipped out of the door, careful not to let any of the puppies escape. I helped her brush straw from her dress, but did not admonish her for the dirtiness of her clothes, for she was so happy, and goodness knew there was little enough joy in her life at the Manor.

Back in the inn we sat down to tea and biscuits with Mr. and Mrs. Greenslade – what Mr. Greenslade cheerfully called 'elevenses' – and I was pleased to see that Sophie remembered her manners. But her thoughts were clearly on the puppies, and when Mr. Greenslade drained his cup and stood up, she looked at me imploringly.

"Go on, then," I said, unable to hide a smile, and she bounded joyfully after the innkeeper.

"Would you like to go for a stroll before luncheon?" Frances asked. "You'll be dining with us, of course?"

"Thank you, that's very kind. And a walk would be lovely."

Frances called one of the serving girls and instructed her to mind the inn while we were out, then we donned hats and coats and ventured into the street. The day was chill but clear, and the wind had not yet grown strong enough to be discomforting. Frances took my arm and we meandered up the main street, stopping now and then to examine the contents of the shop windows. I was not given to spending money on frivolities, but I did like to window-shop now and again, and I was very much enjoying the change in routine. But whenever I looked back towards the sea I saw the island crouched there in the bay, with the old stone house perched atop it, and my thoughts inevitably strayed back to Lucy.

"Why are there no longer any servants at Greythorne Manor?" I asked Frances as we turned off the main street into one of the smaller thoroughfares. "It would make things easier for Jonas, if nothing else."

Frances shook her head. "I'm afraid I don't know," she said. "Lucy only told me that one by one they left, and the Professor was reluctant to replace them."

We walked on in silence for a while, both busy with our own thoughts. Far from giving me the answers I sought, each new thing I learned about Greythorne Manor seemed only to raise further questions. But I was grateful that Frances was so forthcoming, for to me one of the saddest elements of Lucy's story was the reluctance of people to discuss it. From the little I knew of her she had been a bright, charismatic young woman, and it seemed such a shame that her spark of life should be allowed to fade into ignominy when she had done nothing whatsoever to deserve it.

Chapter 13

We continued up the steep main street, passing the old stone church where I'd prayed all those months back. There was little to be seen of Grimly, really, for apart from the inn and the church there was only a narrow strip of shops, the quaint little school and the post office. As we neared the latter Frances paused.

"Do you mind awfully if I just pop in to post a card to my Bess?" she asked. "Arthur and I are traveling down to see her the day after tomorrow, and we'll be there for a month. I just want to let her know the time of our train." She sighed happily. "It'll be the first time in years we've had such a long holiday."

"Of course. I'll wait here – I'd like to look in the milliner's across the street."

I wandered over to the hat shop and perused the bonnets in the window, but found more to interest me in the streetscape and the few people wandering by. Life in Grimly had a constant, gentle rhythm to it that I liked, and I wished the Professor had chosen to take a house on the mainland.

I was so consumed with my own thoughts that I did not notice Frances returning, and jumped when she called my name. With her was a prim, older woman I recognized from church – Miss Sarah Persimmon, the village schoolteacher.

"Sarah, you remember Miss Featherstone?" Frances said to Miss Persimmon, who nodded.

"I'm pleased to see you again, Miss Featherstone." Her manner was very upright and proper; she was the exact opposite of her companion.

"Won't you join us for tea?" Frances asked.

"Why, thank you, that's very kind. And how is Arthur? And Bess?"

We meandered back down the hill towards the inn, the ladies chatting about village minutiae. I half-listened, but I knew none of their subjects, so was free to lose myself in my thoughts.

The tap-room was exactly as we had left it; there were no customers and Sophie and Mr. Greenslade were still preoccupied in the yard. I had the feeling the child would stay with the puppies all night if she were allowed. We settled ourselves before the fire, and Frances rang the bell for tea.

"And how have you settled in to Greythorne Manor, Miss Featherstone?" Miss Persimmon asked, peering at me over her steel-rimmed spectacles.

"Tolerably well, I think, ma'am."

"And Sophie Greythorne is a good pupil?"

"Yes indeed, I've never met a child with such a willingness to learn." I decided not to mention the trouble I'd had with her at the beginning; it seemed unfair to slander Sophie's character so, when she could hardly help the odd environment in which she'd been brought up.

"She sounds just like her mother, then," Miss Persimmon said. "Now there was a lass who could have gone on to great things. She had so much life and potential, and to watch it drain from her was just awful."

"I suppose you knew her well," I said.

"Aye, well enough," Miss Persimmon said. "I was friends with her mother, God rest her, and knew Lucy as an infant, and then when she got older she became one of my pupils. It's a small village, you know, Miss Featherstone."

"So I see, ma'am."

"I had a letter from Winifred Johnston the other day," Miss Persimmon said, turning to Frances. "She's planning to visit in the spring. Her lad Thomas and his wife have just had a baby boy – their first. They've named him George after his grandfather."

"That's wonderful news," Frances said. "I should dearly love to see her again. Mrs. Johnston was the cook at Greythorne Manor for many years," she added, for my benefit, and I felt my eyebrows rising in surprise.

"Aye, that was a strange time," Miss Persimmon said. "I know Win misses Grimly and her friends here, but she's told me time and again she has no regrets about leaving the Manor. There were a lot of odd happenings there, and then poor Lucy's death – I think Win still blames herself a little for it." She shook her head sadly. "She left not long before the poor lass died," she continued, noticing my confusion. "I think she feels that if she'd been there it wouldn't have happened."

"That's ridiculous," Frances said. "It was a tragic accident."

"Aye, I know," Miss Persimmon said. "Or so they say, anyhow. But it must have been odd to live in the midst of it. Lucy did her best to be a good mistress of the house, and I do believe she was happy there for a time, particularly after little Sophie came along. But the loss of her second child hit her hard."

"She lost a baby?" I interjected. The poor, poor woman, to have suffered so.

"Aye," Miss Persimmon said. "She was overjoyed to be pregnant again, but she couldn't – ah …" she lowered her voice "... hold onto the babe, and the Professor was little help. I suppose a man as brilliant as he must be naturally highly focused, but to my mind he neglected her shamefully in favor of those researches of his, and it was no surprise the relationship began to cool. You know, he even forbade her to attend her sister's wedding?"

"Surely not?"

"Yes indeed. But Jonas took Lucy and the little one over anyway, without the Professor's knowledge, and suffered for it too."

"What happened?"

She shrugged. "I don't rightly know, only Win said that the next day poor Jonas could be seen sporting a black eye. To my mind there's far more to the Professor than can be seen at first glance."

She paused and took a sip of her tea.

"Good intellect is nothing without good character," she continued, reminding me vividly of one of the Brookvale mistresses, "and I had my doubts about the Professor right from the start, you'll remember."

"Oh, rubbish," Frances scoffed. "You were as infatuated as the rest of us, as *I* recall. A handsome university man, come to take up residence in the Manor, and with apparently no shortage of means – why, he was the most eligible bachelor in town, even if it all did later prove a sham."

"What do you mean?" I asked.

"Well now, I don't like to speak ill of anyone, and of course I didn't know the details of his finances, but I believe he wasn't as well-off as he first made out," she said. "In the two years or so after Lucy arrived at the Manor, as I told you, a number of the servants left in rather queer circumstances and weren't replaced. It was a rather odd business."

"Why was it odd? Surely any large house has a regular turnover of staff?"

"That's true, of course, but it was the manner in which they left that was odd. In the end it all became too much for Win too, and she had no choice but to resign as well. But I know it was a wrench for her, leaving poor Lucy and the little girl."

"Why didn't he replace the staff?" I asked.

Frances shook her head. "Perhaps he couldn't afford it – that was what I always assumed."

"I don't know," Miss Persimmon said. "I doubt that was the real reason. I remember Win saying that the Professor seemed to be getting increasingly paranoid, thinking that someone was after his precious researches. He had a student over from the university to help him for a while, you know – a young man called Alistair, or Alexander, I think it was. That's right – Alexander Grantham."

"I remember now," Frances interjected. "He stayed the night here. He was a charming young man, rather earnest and very kind."

"He and Lucy became good friends, and I suspect there was deeper feeling than that," Miss Persimmon said, with a suggestive raise of her eyebrows.

"Surely not!" I exclaimed.

"Well now, it wouldn't be the first time a bright young woman, neglected by her husband, had fallen for a lad who showed her kindness," she said, making me wonder if she was not quite the confirmed old spinster I'd first thought. "I don't know how the Professor could have failed to notice it. But she was too smart for infidelity, and too aware of the consequences. She would never have done anything that might have meant losing Sophie."

"So what happened in the end?" By this time I was completely caught up in the story.

"Well, eventually Alexander went away like all the others," Miss Persimmon said. "It wasn't long after Christmas, when Sophie was about two, I think. Actually, it was quite abrupt, as I recall; he just took off one day without a word to anyone but the Professor, it seems. And it wasn't long after that that the staff began to leave."

"What a strange business," Frances said. "I don't believe I've heard you talk of it before."

Miss Persimmon drained her teacup. "I haven't," she said. "Most of it is just second-hand gossip from Win, and you know how I usually feel about gossip. But seeing another bright young woman going to the

Manor – well, one can't help remembering." She laughed. "Aren't we a bunch of silly old folk?" she said. "We shouldn't be boring poor Miss Featherstone with our queer tales. It's just a rundown old house with its fair share of sadness, but there's naught to be afraid of really, I suppose."

She stood up. "In any case, I should be going – Mrs. Morris has invited me to luncheon. Thank you very much for the tea, Frances, and it was a pleasure to see you again, Miss Featherstone. I hope your sojourn at the Manor is a happy one."

"Thank you, Miss Persimmon."

"Well now," Frances said, as the door closed behind the schoolteacher, "fancy that. I've lived here for nigh on thirty years and I'd never heard those stories about Greythorne Manor. It's strange how the place can be so close to the village and yet a world away."

I nodded in understanding.

"I remember first seeing Sophie when she was just a wee thing and they came across for the day with Jonas," Frances continued as we cleared away the tea things. "Lucy was radiant; I've never seen any woman so joyful. But she just adored children, and she would have loved to have had a great brood of them running round, bringing some life back into the old place."

"But she never had any more. Miss Persimmon said she lost a baby?" I could not even imagine the sorrow of a mother who'd lost her child.

"Aye." Frances shook her head sadly. "She was with child again before Sophie was even a year old, but the baby was born very early, and never took a breath, from what little of it Lucy told us. It took her some time to recover – it was there in all in her letters: the grief. She blamed herself, I believe. And then ... well ... relations between her and the Professor began to worsen, and more children ... It became *unlikely* they would add to their brood, if you grasp my meaning."

I flushed, but nodded.

"She adored Sophie," Frances said. "She had so many dreams for her. She wanted her to be well educated, and to not have to rely on marriage for her future prospects as Lucy herself had had to. That's why I'm so glad you're here, and that you've stuck at it. Lucy would have been so proud." Her lips trembled for a moment, then she brushed her hands together, business-like. "I believe that's the luncheon-bell."

Mr. Greenslade and Sophie having been duly summoned, we all sat down to luncheon in the dining room. Sophie was fidgeting with the excitement of being allowed to dine with her elders, until I gave her a stern look and she desisted.

"I hope you haven't been making a nuisance of yourself," I said to her as the meal drew to a close and we rose to take our leave. I should have been keeping a closer eye on her; I had been so engrossed in Lucy's story that I had neglected my duties.

But Mr. Greenslade interjected. "Not at all, miss," he said. "She's been no trouble at all. She's been completely caught up with them puppies. And one of the lads even let her sit on old Copper while he walked her round the yard. I think we've turned her into a budding horsewoman." He rose from the table and we followed.

"I hope you've thanked Mr. Greenslade," I said to Sophie.

"Thank you *so* much," Sophie said, grasping the innkeeper's work-roughened hands in hers. "I've had the most wonderful day."

He patted her head affectionately. "You're welcome, lass. It's been my pleasure."

"We should be going," I said. "We don't want to be late for Jonas." I turned to Frances. "We really have had a wonderful day," I said. "Thank you again for your hospitality."

"You're very welcome," she said, kissing me on both cheeks. "I'm glad we were able to get better acquainted. You know you're welcome here at any time, no matter what." She gave me a shrewd look, and I wondered if she was thinking of Lucy.

Chapter 14

Jonas was already at the boat when we arrived, his sacks of provisions loaded into the stern. He did not ask us about our day; I assumed he did not want to know what we'd been up to. He simply grunted when I attempted to exchange pleasantries, and helped us into the boat.

The voyage back was uneventful. Sophie, worn out with all the excitement, dozed against my shoulder, and even I was too tired to worry much about the waves around the rocks. As the island loomed up before us, however, I remembered the story Miss Persimmon had told me about poor Lucy; I still did not know what to make of it. I pushed it from my mind as the boat ground against the beach, concentrating on waking Sophie and helping her back onto dry land.

When we reached the house Sophie and I went straight to the schoolroom, where we spent the rest of the afternoon in gentle pursuits, alternately reading and playing board games. After an early bread-and-milk supper I tucked her into bed, then sat beside her as she drifted off to sleep.

"It was such a lovely day," she murmured. "I just know I'll have good dreams tonight."

"You must remember not to mention any of this to your father," I said, suddenly fearful we would be found out. "I'm not sure he'd approve."

"I know," she said. "I won't tell." She cuddled her raggedy doll closer, her eyelids fluttering closed. Within minutes she was sound asleep.

I returned to the schoolroom and picked up my mending, but I could not concentrate and found myself having to unpick almost as many stitches as I sewed. Eventually I threw it down in frustration and stood, taking a candle from the mantelpiece. I checked on Sophie and found her sleeping deeply, then crept out into the hallway, drawn inexorably to Lucy's chamber.

I had not been in the bedroom since that fateful day the Professor had happened upon me there, and if he had been in the house I would have continued to avoid it. Perhaps it came of having so lately heard her story, however, but I felt closer to the doomed young woman than I had before, and I wanted to learn all I could about her. Why had she done what she'd done?

The chamber was exactly as I'd found it previously, though the stool before the dressing table lay on its side where I'd upset it in my haste. I walked over and righted it, then sat before the table as I had before. Unsure of what I was looking for, I nevertheless opened the drawers and began to examine their contents. Finding nothing of interest, I turned to the jewelry box. The necklaces and ornaments were as I remembered them; the only thing missing was the jeweled hair ornament the Professor had given me, which I could not bring myself to wear – not that I had had occasion to.

I was about to close the lid of the box when I noticed a small white triangle of paper peeking around the edge of the velvet lining. I slid my fingernail between the edge and bottom of the box, to no avail, but I had more success with one of the jeweled hatpins. Using it as a lever, I discovered the box had a false bottom, so neatly fitted as to be all but invisible. I grasped the edge of the paper and pulled gently so as not to tear it. Unfolding it, I saw it was a letter, in a neat feminine hand, which had clearly never been sent.

28 June 1889

My dear Frances,

I feel I must apologize for the somewhat hysterical tone of my last letter. I have always found the winters here difficult; the howl of the wind preys on the mind.

We had some visitors arrive today, and they are the oddest-looking fellows I ever saw. Jonas rowed the two of them over from the mainland this evening. I was out walking after having put Sophie to bed – for I love the long summer evenings here, where it does not grow dark until late – and as I neared the cove I heard voices. For some reason I decided to make myself scarce, so I crouched behind a boulder on the cliff-top. It was hardly the respectable thing for the lady of the house to do, and I still don't know what prompted such an action; I only knew I did not want to be seen.

The two men had the appearance of undertakers – they were very properly dressed, in top hats and tails, with dark ribbons adorning their headwear. Both were pale in appearance, almost to the point of ghoulishness, as if their skin had never seen sun. There was a long parcel in the boat between them; so long it stretched almost the entire length. It was wrapped in sacking and looked oddly familiar.

As I crouched there puzzling over the mysterious package, I heard a noise behind me. I turned and saw Nathaniel coming down the path towards the boat. Thankfully the path diverted away from my hiding place and I was able to remain unseen. He greeted the men warmly with a handshake, though neither of them returned his friendliness. Nathaniel handed the taller one a bag that looked to me like a money-purse, then, after pocketing it, the fellow gestured to his companion and they hoisted the bundle up onto their shoulders and carried it between them up the slope. I caught snatches of Nathaniel's attempts at conversation: "... glad to do business with you ... invaluable to my research ... hope we can continue to work together ..." but the two men made no reply.

Jonas followed them up the hill, after staying behind a few moments to secure the boat. As he passed he glanced my way, and I felt sure he saw me, for he seemed to look right into my eyes. If he did, however, he made no sign of it, and I will not mention it in case I truly escaped his notice.

It is only as I recount this incident now that a thought occurs to me. I had been feeling sure I had seen a similar mysterious package before, and now I believe I know where. I fear I have been blind to my husband's researches for too long; I must know what it is he does in his laboratory. Tonight I am resolved to wait until all the house is asleep, and then I shall see what I shall see. I will write to you of my findings.

Your affectionate

Lucy

I frowned to myself, reading the last paragraph again. Why had Lucy never sent the letter, and why had she not written to Frances again, as she'd clearly intended to do? What had she found in the cellar?

I folded the paper, my hands trembling. Part of me wished to return to my room and think no more about it, but my mind was racing. It was as if pieces of a puzzle were falling into place before my eyes, and my stomach clenched with fear, for myself and for Sophie.

Using the hatpin again I carefully removed the false bottom, intending to replace the letter, for I did not wish the Professor to know of my discovery should he visit the chamber. It was only as I was peering into the box, trying to slide the document back into place, that I noticed another, smaller piece of paper tucked away in a corner. I caught it with the edge of the pin and pried it loose, then unfolded it with trembling fingers. It was a single sheet ripped hastily from a notebook or diary, dated the day after the previous letter, but with no salutation or farewell. I could not tell if Frances was the intended recipient.

29 June 1889

I cannot stay here. I have tried – God knows, I have tried – but my mind is made up. After what I saw last night I can tarry no longer. Even now, the horror of it rests so greatly upon my soul that I cannot bear to write of it. Suffice it only to say that my husband's researches are not as benign as I once thought; he is dabbling with the very essence of life itself, and he knows not what he does. It is ghastly; it is inhuman. I am revolted and I will not allow my daughter to grow up in such a place. I know what the consequences will be if I leave, and my mother would undoubtedly tell me to stay and do my duty. But I swear, if he were beating me I would not be as hasty to go as I am now. Even if it means my family disowning me, and having to make my own way in the world, then so be it. Poverty I believe I can endure, but this devilish work I cannot. This place is cursed and I will not stay a moment longer. Tonight I will take Sophie and make for the boat, and we will either reach safety or die in the attempt. Farewell to this accursed rock and all its inhabitants, living and dead, forever.

Chapter 15

I sat staring at the slip of paper, my hands shaking. Lucy could not have known the fate to which she was condemning herself, in spite of her brave, terribly prescient words, but one thing was clear to me – she had not taken her own life. Perhaps it had been a tragic accident; perhaps not. In any case, the cause was immaterial. Lucy had died and all her dreams for Sophie had died with her.

I could not bear to stay in the room a moment longer, so I replaced the papers in the jewelry box, ensuring all was left as I had first encountered it, then took the candle and returned to my chamber. Sophie was still sleeping soundly, so I banked up the schoolroom fire and sought my own bed.

I was bone-weary, but as soon as I found myself in bed I could not rest. What had Lucy discovered to cause such a violent reaction? Something intimately connected with the Professor's researches, of which I still knew little, but what? Were Sophie and I even now in danger?

This was the thinking of a loon, I reasoned to myself. Perhaps Lucy had simply been of a hysterical temperament, and had seen something she had misunderstood. But she did not seem that sort; her words were clear and well reasoned. She was not a woman to be easily shaken, I thought.

Sleep eventually claimed me despite the swirling torrent of my thoughts, though my dreams were restless and populated by ghouls and half-imagined apparitions. In the morning I woke grumpy and tired, but Sophie was in a fine mood, still having not got over the excitement of the previous day's adventures. It was difficult to convince her to sit down to her lessons, but eventually she quieted and bent over her books. A fine misty rain had appeared mid-morning, and the light in the schoolroom was grey and sparkling, as if caught inside a cobweb. It was so dim I was forced to light the lamp, and it seemed there would be no going out today.

In the afternoon, however, the mist burned off, leaving the day bright and sunny. After our luncheon Sophie and I took our drawing materials and ventured outside, for I felt restless and agitated, and hoped the fresh air would clear my head. It was unseasonably warm, even with the sea breeze, and we perched on a handy outcrop of rocks on the cliff-top, where we could look back over the island to the sweep of the pine forest and the house rising up like a monolith behind it. I set Sophie to sketching the landscape, and arranged my own drawing board, but I could not concentrate on art. From where I sat I could see Lucy's memorial stone, and I kept thinking of her final words: *Farewell to this accursed rock and all its inhabitants, living and dead, forever.*

"What are you drawing?"

Sophie and I both jumped near clean out of our skins.

"Professor!" I gasped, rising with what I hoped was a modicum of decorum. "I didn't realize you had returned." Thank heaven he had not done so the day before!

He flashed his handsome smile. "I've only just arrived. Jonas is taking my things to the house, but I thought I'd come and see how my girls are getting on." He bent down and kissed Sophie – the first real sign of affection I could recall him showing her.

"Have you missed me?" he asked.

"Of course, sir. Did you have a good trip?" He had returned much sooner than I had expected, but I did not say so.

"It was … productive, yes. Have you done anything interesting in my absence?"

"Nothing to speak of, sir – just our normal lessons." I hoped Sophie would remember my entreaties not to speak of our outing to the village, and indeed she did not seem inclined to talk of it. Instead, she held her out her sketchbook.

"It's the house, Papa," she said. "See, here's the forest, and there's the house."

The Professor bent over her work, scrutinizing it. "Your perspective is wrong," he said. "The house ought not to be that tall." Sophie's shoulders slumped, but she said nothing.

"Miss Featherstone," he said, turning to me, "perhaps you would do me the honor of dining with me tonight?"

"Of course, sir."

"Good." Then without another word he turned and strode across the rocky headland, back towards the house. I took a deep breath to slow my racing heart and clenched my hands to stop them shaking, for I could not let my young charge see how unnerved I was.

"Now then, Sophie," I said, "let's take a look at this drawing."

*

Dinner with the Professor was rather awkward on my part, for I was having difficulty reconciling the congenial, charming man before me with the accounts of Lucy's mercurial and violent husband, despite having witnessed his rages first-hand. I found myself much distracted, and began to wonder if delving into Lucy's history had been a mistake.

The Professor seemed keen to talk – after all, it had been some time since our last meal together, and perhaps even he hankered for company from time to time – and I was content with his rather didactic, one-sided conversation. He required little response from me, and that suited my current mood perfectly, but I could see how it would frustrate a bright, opinionated young woman like Lucy. I felt as if the solid ground was being swept from under me, leaving me all at sea. I escaped the meal as quickly as politeness would allow, and returned to my haven in the schoolroom.

*

The feeling of discombobulation did not vanish with sleep, but persisted throughout the next day; it was as if the Professor's return had swept away any certainty I had left. In the afternoon I sent Sophie out to play in the sunshine and went down to the library, seeking solace, for I knew not what to do. It was bathed in sunlight from the enormous windows; shafts of it slanted through the dusty air, creating sparkling, ethereal roads leading skyward. The books in their leather bindings glowed red and blue and green like long-forgotten jewels. I wandered idly along the upper gallery, choosing books at random and flicking through them, but I could not concentrate. In the dusty half-light I thought more than once that I glimpsed the figure of a young woman moving among the shelves. It was simply a trick of the light and my overactive imagination, but it left me feeling still more unsettled.

Back upstairs, I sat before the schoolroom fire, my sewing on my knee, musing. Shortly afterwards, I heard Sophie returning from outside. I greeted her and helped her out of her coat and hat, ushering her to stand in front of the fire that was crackling merrily in the grate.

"Did you have a nice afternoon?" I asked. She just nodded. Since her father's return, Sophie's manner had become more subdued; she was again complaining of nightmares and seemed pale and tired. I knew not to what to attribute it, for even now – with perhaps willful blindness – I refused to give weight to my suspicions. She seemed healthy enough in body, but her spirit was much depressed. I was at a loss as to how I could help her, save to let her lose herself in work and play, and to love her with some shadow of motherliness. I could never replace Lucy, nor did I seek to, but I could not help feeling she would have wanted her daughter to be cared for, and the Professor seemed incapable of providing such affection.

Sophie ate her dinner listlessly, then complained of a headache and retired early to bed. I was worried for her, but hoped her ailments would be eased by a good night's sleep, untroubled by nightmares. She seemed to fall asleep easily enough, and I returned to my sewing. When, however, I retired to my own bed some hours later, sleep would not come to me. The wind had picked up and was wuthering round the house once more, howling with the grief of a thousand lost souls. Pulling the covers up to my ears, I wondered if Lucy's was among them.

Chapter 16

I was tossing and turning, tangling myself in the sheets in my agitation, when I thought I heard a creak. I lay still, listening, and heard it again: the familiar groan of Sophie's bedroom door. I sprang out of bed, pulling on my dressing gown and slippers, but did not take a candle. I was not sure why such a stealthy instinct possessed me, but I knew I did not wish to be seen.

Creeping through the schoolroom, part of me scoffed at the situation; after all, it was probably just the wind. The door between the schoolroom and Sophie's room was ajar, so I peered carefully round it, expecting to find my charge asleep in her bed and the door to the hallway blowing in a draught. But as I looked, I saw in the silvery moonlight the shadow of a man; he was just leaving through the outer door, and he carried the unmistakable shape of a sleeping child in his arms. I wondered how it was she did not wake.

A kind of manic frenzy seized me then. My first thought was to scream, and if there had been a household to wake I would have, but there wasn't. There was only me, all alone, and if anything was to be done to save Sophie from the clutches of whatever evil held her I would have to do it myself.

"Help me, Lucy," I whispered, then, after allowing a few seconds to elapse to ensure I would not be heard, I slipped through Sophie's room and after the intruder.

My eyes had adjusted to the darkness by now, and I was able to see quite clearly in the trickle of moonlight that made its way into the corridor. The bulk of the man was some distance ahead of me, and even as I watched he turned a corner and I lost sight of him. I hurried after, taking care that my footsteps should make as little noise as possible.

The chase led me deep into the twisting maze of the Manor's hallways and back rooms, up and down short staircases and, it felt, around in circles, until I had completely lost my bearings. I wondered why the man was taking such a circuitous route, but perhaps that was simply the nature of the strange old house. I was reminded suddenly of my early days here, exploring with Sophie.

This thought must have triggered something in my memory, for the grey stone walls seemed to grow suddenly familiar. I realized we were come to the outer wall of the house, far away from Sophie's and my apartments. And as the tower loomed up before me, I knew at last where I was, and what lay below – as I had hardly allowed myself to fear, we were approaching the Professor's laboratory.

The intruder barely stopped for the tower door, pushing his way through it with enough force that it did not swing to again. I lurked in the hallway, watching from a distance, my heart thundering in my ears. The thought of descending those dark stone steps to confront I-knew-not-what made my knees tremble, but I could not let Sophie face whatever it was alone. At last I understood the poor child's 'nightmares', and cursed myself for failing to believe sooner what my intuition had been clamoring for me to understand. But what was the reason behind it all? Why snatch a little girl from her bed in the middle of the night? There was only one place I could possibly find the answers, so I crept through the tower door and gingerly descended the steep stone stairs.

The spiral staircase was tight and seemed to go on forever; I was soon dizzy. I could feel myself descending into hell, and it took all my willpower to take the next step. If it hadn't been for Sophie I know my courage should have failed me entirely and I would have run back to my bed as fast as I could, for I am not naturally brave. My pace was agonizingly slow, as there was no light in the staircase; I was forced to find my way by touch, grasping the wall with one hand while carefully feeling with my foot for the next step. I began to wonder if I had stumbled into some sort of nightmare – the kind so vivid as to seem real – and if I would wake shortly in my bed and scoff at my silly fears. But I did not wake.

There was no sign of the man now; he and Sophie had vanished. I presumed his familiarity with the staircase made his going easier and faster than mine, though my steps were also slowed by the fear of bumping into him in the dark.

I rounded another bend and blinked: a faint glow emanated up into the stairwell. At first I thought it was just my eyes playing tricks, but with each step the light increased, and I realized it was coming from whatever room lay at the bottom of the stairs. We were well underground by now; Greythorne Manor evidently had deep cellars, its foundations buried at the island's rocky heart. I had expected it to be cold, but oddly enough I grew warmer as I went. I reasoned to myself that the temperature in the cellars would be relatively even all year round, and as it was so cold outside at present it would naturally feel warm below. The simple logic helped calm me.

I felt for the next step, but my foot found only flat ground. I took a deep breath, unsure of what I would be walking into. Light flooded through the doorway at the bottom of the stairs, coming, I could see, from an oil lamp standing on a bench. Carefully I peered round the door frame, trying to see without being seen, and had to stifle a gasp so loud I was afraid I had given myself away.

The door opened onto a long, large stone room, cluttered with all manner of scientific equipment. There were tall glass jars and vials spread across benches, and some sort of wire-filled device which was draped, spider-like, on a workbench, and appeared to my untutored mind to have something to do with electricity. And in the middle of the room Sophie lay on a table that was covered with a sheet; the kind a doctor would use. She appeared to be unconscious, while Jonas was drawing blood from the crook of her right elbow with a needle and glass syringe. I thought again of Sophie's "nightmares". How long had they been doing this to her?

But then my gaze shifted to the table beside her, and I retched in horror, for on it lay the desiccated body of Lucy Greythorne. She had clearly been embalmed, and the process had preserved her features in an eerie likeness of life, right down to her fair hair, but there was no sense of *her*, nothing to link this mummified corpse with the pretty young woman in the drawing-room picture.

I was shaking by now; how in that moment I wished I had remained ignorant of such things – that

I had never come to this infernal place. The stone I had seen on the cliff was not a grave-marker, but only a memorial – Lucy had never lain there. She had instead been held in stasis for God only knew what reason, denied escape even in death. I prayed that her soul at least was at peace. But what manner of evil was playing out here, in the depths of the earth? I peered out further, trying to get a sense of the wider room.

"Ah, Miss Featherstone," a smooth voice said from behind me, "so glad you could join us." My hands were pulled roughly behind my back and I was manhandled out into the light. I screamed loud and long, forgetting there was no one to hear.

"Now then," said the Professor – for of course it was he – "stop that. You don't want me to gag you, do you?" I shook my head silently. "Good girl. Now, get onto that table." He pointed to a third table, the same as the other two, on the far side of the corpse (for I could not think of those remains as *Lucy*). I scrambled up, as undignified as it was, for I was terrified of the fire blazing in his eyes.

"What are you going to do to me?" I whispered. He merely smiled and turned away; I imagined it was the same kind of grin a wolf would give a sheep. I looked over at Sophie across the body of her mother. Jonas had finished his work, and was carrying two vials of blood across the room to a workbench covered in a forest of scientific-looking glassware.

"Sophie!" I hissed, but she did not respond. I began to shake again as I saw she was tied to the bench with thick leather straps. Then Jonas came over to me, and I realized what he meant to do.

"No!" I pleaded, beginning, I am ashamed to say, to cry. "No, please don't!" But he was immune to my supplications, and buckled my arms and legs to the table just like Sophie's. I was trapped. I struggled fiercely as a wave of panic overtook me, but it was useless.

"What are you going to do to me?" I asked again as the Professor returned to my side. He shook his head at me as if I were an ignorant child.

"Oh, Nell, Nell," he said. "May I call you Nell? I'm not going to *do* anything to you. *We're* going to make history – together. We spoke once of being collaborators, did we not? You will be giving life to another; the first woman to do so without experiencing the miracle of birth. Is that not a great honor?"

"I don't understand." I was breathing deeply, trying to fight off waves of terror-induced nausea. Was he going to kill me?

"Of course you don't, dear Nell," he said, with a paternalistic smile. "No one else does. Lucy didn't – it was a great pity. I told you my research fields were biology and anatomy, but I failed to mention that I am specifically interested in reanimation and galvanism. Are you familiar with the work of Giovanni Aldini?"

I shook my head, feeling like I was swimming through a dream.

The Professor sighed. "A shame, particularly for one purporting to be so interested in science. His work on galvanism was groundbreaking, and of much inspiration to me. And yet he never mastered what I have managed to, so I suppose that makes me the greater scientist in the end."

This last was said in perfect seriousness, without a trace of humility, and I could only stare.

"What do you mean?" He clearly wanted me to ask, and the longer he talked, the more time I had to assess the situation.

He smiled. "Not so long ago I had a breakthrough. After many years of hard work, and many failures, I discovered a way to transfer the life-force from one living to one deceased, and constructed a machine to allow me to do so." He pointed to the heap of wires I had noticed earlier.

"That's impossible!"

"On the contrary, my dear. I have proven it several times over to be possible, though in my early experiments it was difficult to get the reanimation to hold for longer than a few days."

"But why do you need me and Sophie?" I was playing for time, trying to keep him talking – anything to stop him touching that dreadful machine. Then, suddenly, it was as if a veil had been drawn from before my eyes, and the whole grisly business became clear.

"You're using Sophie to reanimate Lucy's body?" I gasped. "The mother lives in the child? You loved her so much you couldn't ever bear to let her go?" My mind was racing; I was sure I had unraveled the mystery that had been plaguing me all these months.

But the Professor threw back his head and laughed: a deep, booming laugh with a slightly unhinged edge. "Bravo, Miss Featherstone," he said, clapping in mock appreciation. "But if this is an example of the spirit of analysis and enquiry you bring then I would advise you to stay well away from the scientific disciplines."

For the first time I felt a lurch of uncertainty. I glanced across at the corpse, and at Sophie sprawled on the table. "I don't understand."

"My dear Nell, it's all perfectly simple," he said. "I'm not using Sophie to reanimate her mother; the child is the one who has been reanimated. It has held for five years now; she is my greatest experiment. I test her blood regularly, and the process shows no signs of failing – with careful maintenance, of course."

I felt the world begin to spin. There was a metallic taste in my mouth, and I feared I should faint or be sick. Sophie, little Sophie, grown so dear to me, was *dead*? Or not even dead, but something else entirely?

"Lucy knew what you were doing," I said, as understanding flared like a gas lamp. She had discovered something in the laboratory that she could not countenance, something that had fueled her decision to leave. It was all beginning to make sense.

"She happened upon my research," he said, "but it was still at a primitive stage and she did not take the time to understand it properly. And yet, as it has played out, she has gone on to provide me with arguably the greatest scientific discovery since Galileo. That night, I followed her to try and explain, but she would not listen. She ran from me, and then she fell." His expression was that of a wounded child.

"When I reached them the child was already dead. Lucy was badly injured – she was barely breathing – and Sophie had fallen on top of her. The shock of the fall had killed the girl, for she was only small, but she was otherwise unharmed. At first I was overwhelmed with grief, remembering how my dear mother was similarly snatched from me, but then I realized that this was a once-in-a-lifetime chance to test my ideas on blood relationships and reanimation." There was fervor in his eyes, and his voice was filled with passion for his subject. "You see, prior to that, the longest reanimation I had managed was two weeks, and it had given me cause to think about the relationship between the source body and the subject being reanimated. I had a feeling that a reanimation using blood relatives would be more successful. Lucy was already near death; what better way to leave this earth than to save your own flesh and blood while doing so? I knew she would appreciate the sacrifice. So I brought my daughter back to me, and she has lived the life of a normal human child for nearly half a decade. When I introduce her to the world she will make me famous."

I shook my head mutely, but he seemed blind to my horror, caught up as he was in extolling his own genius.

"The brilliance, of course," he continued, "is not just that I successfully reanimated Sophie, but that it's lasted as long as it has. After the initial transfer of life-force, I pioneered a medicine, made from the traces of essences found in Lucy's blood, which allows the reanimation to be maintained. There is just one final part of the experiment to conduct before the research is ready to be published, and then all those university naysayers who told me it would never amount to anything will be forced to eat their words. They ran me out of town, but I shall have the last laugh."

"What is this experiment?" Even as the words passed my lips I dreaded asking them; I had a feeling I would not like the answer.

"Corpses have a finite life, ironically," he said. "One can revisit the same body only so many times for use in reanimation. Lucy has served me well over the last five years, but her biological reserves are all but exhausted. It is now time to see whether my methods have been refined enough that any person, even one with no biological connection to the subject, can be used to maintain the reanimation of another. I wanted a young woman in the prime of life, of similar age and temperament to Lucy, and since Sophie was at the age at which she required a governess, it was the perfect opportunity. I had hoped this young lady would be someone after my own heart – intelligent, well versed in the natural sciences, and keen to effect a lasting change to society: someone who understood the value of this research and the sacrifices that must be made for it – a collaborator, if you will. It was almost too much to hope for that this woman would be everything I expected and more, but when you arrived all my dreams came true." He stroked the side of my face and I shuddered.

"Are you going to kill me?"

He shook his head sadly. "Nell, Nell. Is it not the greatest, most noble sacrifice to give your life in exchange for another's? Sophie cannot survive without the medicine I make from Lucy's extracts. With your sacrifice she will go on to live many more fruitful years, to be a woman of refinement and learning, a marvel of the age. Not only that, but I am also pioneering technology that will allow life-force to be stored; I will first extract it from you for use in later investigations, and then I will obtain your essences for Sophie's medicine. Imagine being the pivotal point of two such unprecedented experiments – can't you see what a wonderful future you will be a part of?"

I could not speak; I just turned my face away, unable to look at him. The bile was rising in my throat.

"Now, enough talking," he said abruptly. He walked over to the spidery machine and began unspooling wires from it; he attached them by means of small suction pads to my temples and the tips of my fingers. I began to shake all over, for I knew I must surely die tonight, and to be confronted so baldly with that knowledge is a fearsome thing.

The Professor flipped a switch on the machine, and I braced myself for great pain, but nothing happened. Jonas stared from across the room but remained silent. The Professor's thunderous brows narrowed as he flicked the switch again: still nothing. He growled to himself.

"I must check the connections," he snapped to Jonas. "Watch her!" He turned on his heel and strode to the back of the room, where another doorway branched off into what I assumed must be more cellars. Over on the other table, Sophie began to moan.

Jonas came over to me to check the wiring on my head and hands, but as he did so I grabbed his wrist and would not let him go. "Jonas, please!" I implored him. "Don't let him do this! You have to help me!" He said nothing, only shook his head, but still I held him tight; fear had put iron into my grip.

"You loved Lucy, didn't you?" I guessed desperately. "You know she wouldn't want this!"

I finally seemed to get through to him, for he looked at me, and now I saw the full force of sadness and longing deep in his grey eyes. Then his gaze sharpened, as if he'd made a decision.

"You're right," he said. "She wouldn't." He began pulling the wires off my fingers and unbuckling the straps, and in less than a minute I was free. In my joy I kissed him quickly on the cheek, then ran to Sophie's side. The buckles were stiff and difficult to undo with my shaking hands, but I was determined not to leave without her. Whatever else she might have been, she was still under my care. I touched her face and she groaned, blinking blearily.

"It's all right, darling," I whispered. "I'm here."

She stared at me in mute terror, and then her eyes widened at something over my shoulder.

"*What are you doing?*" the Professor bellowed, returning from the far cellar and seeing me free. "Jonas! How did this happen?" But Jonas had absented himself; I could catch no sight of him. I fumbled more frantically at Sophie's restraints and she began to whimper. The Professor came striding through the cellar; in desperation I picked up the oil lamp and threw it towards him as hard as I could. It hit the machine and shattered, spraying its contents across the room. Flames began to lick at the coils and vessels and caught the sheets on the table, spreading along the wires still attached to Lucy's corpse. Whatever chemicals had been used to preserve the body only added fuel, and, even in the seconds I spared to watch, her clothes and hair caught fire, giving her a funeral pyre fit for a Viking queen.

The conflagration was enough to distract the Professor momentarily; he dived in and attempted to salvage his precious machine. The last of the straps imprisoning Sophie came free; I snatched her up and ran toward the stairs. The acrid smell of smoke rolled up the stairwell behind us, stinging my nose and throat and making me cough. The fire had taken hold, fueled by the stores of chemicals that lined the cellar walls, and it seemed as if the whole room was aflame. I could not discern the Professor's fate, but I knew that if it were in his power he would soon be after us, and terror put haste into my steps.

Sophie was still weak and disoriented, and clearly in no state to walk, so I continued to carry her. But when we reached the top of the stairs, to my horror I found the heavy oak door closed. I tried the handle but it would not budge. Perhaps it had swung shut in the wind; perhaps the Professor had somehow closed it after I came through; perhaps Jonas on his way out had decided to be quit of the lot of us and locked us in. Whatever the reason, there was no escape that way. I did not know my way through the cellars, either, and in any case they were barred by the Professor and the fire.

I was at the end of my tether, but could not let Sophie see my distress. I sat her down on the steps and leaned against the wall, telling her I was just trying to catch my breath. The air was becoming warm and bitter with smoke; we would soon be overcome with it, if the Professor did not find us first. Then I heard the noise I dreaded: the sound of footsteps pounding up the stairs. I rose to my feet, my heart thundering, looking frantically around for some means of escape, even though I knew it to be futile. The steps were getting closer. I touched the wall, stifling a smoke-induced cough; and suddenly it all came back to me.

"Sophie!" I hissed, bending down and shaking her shoulders. "The secret passage entrance – where is it?" She was almost catatonic with shock, staring into space. I slapped her face – not hard, but with enough force to rouse her and let me communicate what I wanted. She looked at me with reproach in her big brown eyes, but scrambled to her feet. She felt along the wall behind the tapestry and pressed a stone; the false section of wall slid back just as I remembered it, and we scrambled through as the Professor rounded the corner. His blue eyes were blazing and his hair was wild; he looked like a very demon from hell itself. Sophie screamed, but I ignored her and felt for the lever that closed the wall. I found it just as he reached out to us; the panel slid back into place, almost trapping his fingers, and for the moment, at least, we were safe.

"Come on, Sophie," I urged her, grabbing her hand. "You need to be brave now." I did not tell her I already counted her one of the bravest souls of my acquaintance, simply for surviving this long.

We stumbled along in the dark, stubbing our toes and going far slower than I would have wished, but there was nothing for it but to keep on and hope he didn't find some other way in. Sophie knew the passage well and seemed to have the eyesight of a cat, so I let her lead, keeping a tight hold of her hand. The journey seemed even longer than it had the first time I had done it, but at last we reached the corner where the walls branched off at right angles.

"Do you remember?" Sophie whispered. It was the first thing she'd said since our ordeal began.

"I think so," I said, feeling for the corner of the wall. I found it then counted five up and ten across, just as she'd taught me. My fingers brushed the rough grooves of the carven X, and I pressed it; the wall slid back and we tumbled out into cool air and freedom.

Chapter 17

The clouds hung low in the sky above us; a chill wind was rising. We were both clad only in our nightclothes, though I had on a dressing gown, and mercifully we both wore slippers. But winter had already come to this isolated northern rock, and I realized our next danger was death from exposure. I knew what we must do, but the thought terrified me; the only thing worse was the thought of returning to the Manor. That possibility was closed to us after the night's events – now we must run as far and as fast as we could, and hope that God had mercy on us.

Sophie had begun to cry, perhaps from the shock of it all. I crouched down to her level. "Look at me, Sophie," I said. "Tell me what's wrong." I was quite stern with her, but we did not have time for niceties, not if we wished to escape with our lives. I would not think about what the Professor had revealed about her – not yet.

"Don't make me go back there," she begged. "Not back to *him*. Every night they come for me ..." She began to sob more loudly and I held her close.

"Hush now," I said. "I'm not making you go back. In fact, we're going to leave this place for good. But I'll need you to help me. You'll have to be strong. Can you do that?"

She gulped and nodded, wiping her eyes with the back of her hand.

"Good girl," I said, relieved. "Now quickly, let's go." I took her hand and we dashed away, down towards the beach. For a second, in the darkness, I almost thought I saw Lucy, running with a much smaller Sophie clutched in her arms; running from what I had not seen until it was nearly too late.

The fire seemed to have escaped the cellars, perhaps catching hold of the tapestries in the stairwell, for the windows of the Manor were now glowing with fiendish light. I wondered if it was wicked of me to hope the Professor had perished in the conflagration. The wind was beginning to pick up, and every now and then I could have sworn I heard footfalls behind us, but when I turned to look there was nothing. I dragged Sophie along as fast as she could go, and soon we reached the cliff-top above the beach where the boat lay.

"Hurry down, Sophie," I said, ushering her down the narrow path, for there was only room for one at a time. As she did, I glanced back over my shoulder. I jumped, thinking I saw a dark figure outlined against the flames of the house, but I could not be certain. The sight, however, was enough to galvanize me into action, and I hastened after Sophie, determined not to meet the same fate as her mother.

Luck, it seemed, was on our side; the boats were drawn up in their usual spot, and appeared undamaged by the recent bad weather. Between us we managed to haul one down to the water's edge, the wind whipping our hair and blowing salt spray into our faces.

"You'll never get through the rocks," a voice said.

I spun around in terror, fearing it was the Professor, but standing on the beach was Jonas, a sack over his shoulder. I had not heard him arrive over the wind.

"We'll be fine," I said, though in my heart I knew he was right. But what choice did we have?

"You'll surely die."

"Far better to die an honest death at sea than at the hands of the Professor." I intended to sound brave, but could not keep my voice from shaking. Was Jonas going to haul us back bodily to that fearsome laboratory? Or was his plan simply to keep us there until the Professor came for us?

"Stand aside," he said, marching toward the boat.

"What …?"

"I'll row you. It's the only way. Get in while I hold her steady."

"I don't understand."

He looked at me stonily, but could not hide the aching sadness in his eyes. "There was a night like this a long time ago," he said. "It's what I should have done then. Now get in."

I lifted Sophie into the boat before clambering in myself. Jonas shoved it as hard as he could out toward the breakers, then jumped in, getting wet to the knees in the process, and scrambled to unhitch the oars. The breakers crashed over the bow, threatening to swamp us. Had I had time to think, I should have been frozen with fear; as it was I had developed a ruthless single-mindedness. We managed to get the oars over the side, Jonas and I taking one each, and pulled as hard as we could until we were clear of the breakers. We were still being tossed in the swell, but were not now in immediate danger of drowning. I had not thought to ask Sophie if she could swim. I hoped I would not need to find out.

The water was swirling and boiling round the rocks; the wind whipped my hair into my face and sprayed us with salt and foam. The journey across the short strait felt like the longest of my life. Jonas periodically yelled instructions, but apart from this nobody spoke. After we were through the worst of the rocks, but long before we were close to land, my arms and back began to shriek with pain. I wanted only to stop and lie down, but there was nothing for it but to keep going. The swell was getting larger, and more than once the boat lurched and nearly capsized, but each time it mercifully righted itself at the last minute. Sophie said nothing throughout the whole ordeal, but in any case the noise from wind and sea swept words away as soon as they were uttered.

Just when I thought I could go on no longer I glanced over my shoulder and saw the beach rearing before us, the little whitewashed houses of Grimly rising above it. We were some distance from the quay, but that did not matter; I figured we would have a better chance of landing safely on the beach itself. Jonas pointed the nose of the boat directly at the strip of sand and we pulled as hard as we could. The boat was picked up by the surf and propelled hellishly fast toward the beach, but as the bows ground onto land it was caught by the waves and spun round, hurling us overboard into waist-deep water. I scrambled up and grabbed Sophie, who was screaming and crying; as I had thought, she could not swim. I pulled her up the beach and momentarily contemplated returning for the boat – though I could not be sure I had the strength in my arms to haul it up – but it had been caught by the undertow and was already being swept back out to sea. I shrugged it off; it had got us where we needed to be.

Jonas had been badly knocked about by the wave; he lay in the shallows, unmoving. I ran down to him and tugged frantically at his arm; he raised his head and scrambled out of reach of the breakers, looking utterly spent, before falling back onto the sand. In his eyes there was something chilling – a complete absence of hope – and I doubt he would have moved without my coaxing.

I collapsed next to Sophie on the beach, wrapping my arms around her. She was shivering and still crying, and I knew we would need to recover our strength a little before we ventured any further. I took some deep breaths, trying to stave off the shock, for we were not safe yet. Away across the bay, Greythorne Manor burned like a beacon, lighting up the stormy sky.

Jonas staggered up the beach to where we sat; I noticed he still had the sack tied across his shoulders and wondered how it had survived. He unhitched the sodden bag and handed it to me; it was surprisingly heavy.

"What's this?" I asked.

"Medicine for the lass," he muttered. "Should keep her going for about six months. After that …" He shrugged.

I didn't know what to say; I had not had time to fully comprehend the Professor's revelations, nor what they meant for Sophie and for me. But if it was all true, then Jonas had bought the child some precious time.

"Thank you," I said stiffly. "And for the boat … you're right … we wouldn't have survived without you."

He shrugged again. "Least I could do. I've a lot to atone for."

I stood up, looking him in the eye. "He made you do it."

Jonas shook his head sadly. His shoulders sagged; he looked broken and twice his age. "Nay, miss," he said. "I don't deserve your pity, nor your mercy; I should have spoken up long ago. But instead I let all them awful things happen to the mistress, and the little girl, and that poor lad."

For a minute I was unsure to whom he was referring, and then I realized.

"You mean Alexander Grantham?"

He nodded.

"You killed him?"

"I held him down."

"And then the Professor used a corpse he'd bought to reanimate him – and that was what Lucy saw?" I should have been horrified, but after the night's events I felt only numb.

He nodded again.

"It was easy work to begin with," he said, "back in the university days. Decent pay and a bit of respect – two things I'd never had. For a time I truly thought we was going to change the world, like he said. And by the time we came here things was so far gone I hardly noticed. It wasn't until you arrived … And now how can I ever be forgiven?"

"God always forgives," I said, but he shook his head.

"I know where I'll be going, lass. Best place for the likes of me." He had been growing more and more distressed as he spoke; now he tugged distractedly at his hair so that it stood up in tangled corkscrews. Tears glinted on his cheeks; I had never seen the collected, taciturn Jonas so distraught, but he was beyond comfort. Instinctively I reached for his arm, but he brushed me aside, turning back to the sea and the eerie glow of the Manor on the horizon. He began walking down the beach, almost as if his legs were carrying him involuntarily. I glanced at Sophie, who was shivering, hunched up with her arms wrapped round her knees and her face buried, then rose to hurry after him.

"What are you doing, Jonas?" I asked, for he was already standing in ankle-deep water. "The boat is gone. You can't swim back to the Manor!"

He glanced back at me, continuing to walk further into the water. "Aye, miss," he said. "I can't swim at all."

"No!" I cried, the wind sweeping my words away. I stumbled after him, but a wave knocked me off my feet and I sat down hard in the shallows. The wind whipped my hair into my eyes, and my skirts tangled round my legs, hampering my recovery. By the time I struggled to my feet, he was gone.

Chapter 18

I stood there for some minutes, the water lapping at my ankles, my body racked with sobs so violent I feared I should be sick. The image of Jonas walking into the sea was seared into my mind. I know not how long I remained there, only that I began to develop a growing awareness of the cold. I wiped my dripping eyes and nose and clambered back up the beach, picking up the sack and coaxing Sophie to her feet, and looked away towards the village. It was still black night, and would be for some hours, and we could not stay outside. I chewed my lip, contemplating our options. The Greenslades were away visiting Bess, and I could not bear to ask anyone else in Grimly for shelter lest the Professor find us there; I did not know whom I could trust, for our story was quite unbelievable. It was terribly cold, but it seemed our only choice was to lurk in the village for few hours, then catch a train somewhere safer – though no: I had no money. I took a deep breath, trying to keep myself from despair.

Thinking of the train took me back to my journey, all those months earlier, and so I remembered Elsie Drabble and her kind offer of hospitality. I struggled to remember the directions she had given me, but slowly they came limping back: Lark Hill Farm, on the Grimly–Little Norton road. I was unsure in which direction Little Norton lay, but Grimly was small, and I did not doubt we would find the road without too much difficulty.

Mercifully we were spared a difficult climb up the cliffs, for we had only to walk along the beach until it met a set of stairs near the quay. It was further than it looked, however, and by the time we reached the steps Sophie was hangdog and miserable, though she uttered not a word of complaint. She held my hand tightly as we climbed the steep wooden stairs and found ourselves on the fishy-smelling stone quay.

"Are you all right, Sophie?" I asked as we turned into the village's sloping main street. She just nodded, though she looked terribly weary.

"We're going to have to walk a bit further," I said, "but then you'll be able to have a wash and sleep in a bed." She nodded again. I did not tell her that I had no idea how far we had to go, or even whether Elsie and her husband were at home; I hoped they had not gone to town.

We climbed the steep main street to the outskirts of Grimly, past the inn and the quaint little houses all shuttered and dark. At the entrance to the village the road diverged, with a signpost planted at the fork like a sentinel. The right branch read *Grimly Station, 3 miles*, while the left proclaimed *Little Norton, 6 miles*. I sighed with relief.

"Not far now, sweetheart," I told Sophie, though in truth I had no idea how far it was to the farm. Sophie, pale and exhausted, said nothing. We trudged on through the night, shivering in our thin nightclothes, our feet stinging and aching. The night was growing clearer; the wind was dropping and the clouds were parting until they were only ragged skeins strewn across a blanket of stars. For the first time that night the moon shone out, giving us enough light to see by. Although it was a mercy to be no longer buffeted by the wind, as the sky grew clearer the temperature also fell. I bade Sophie hurry, for brisk walking at least helped us to stay warm.

The road ran through fields lined with dry-stone walls, but there were no sheep to be seen; they had all retreated to the little covered shelters that dotted the pastures. It would be tough work farming this area in the depths of winter, but I supposed folk round here were used to it. It certainly explained their hardiness.

Now that my mad instinct for flight was wearing off, I too was growing weary. It became an immense effort simply to continue putting one foot in front of the other, and the road seemed to stretch on interminably. I know not how far we walked – several miles at least, it seemed – but eventually we crested a rise and looked down upon a little vale, in which nestled a dear white farmhouse. My heart was cheered at the sight of it. I took Sophie's hand and we hurried down the hill with renewed vigor in our steps.

A wide-barred wooden gate opened onto the road, with *Lark Hill Farm* painted on it in white. My knees began to shake with relief; at last we were safe. I unlatched the gate and ushered Sophie through, making sure to close it behind me. The house was tucked away at the end of a long, rutted track; at this time of year the wheel-ruts had hardened and we had to be careful where we put our feet. It was slow going, but we managed it without injury, and soon found ourselves at the door of the small white farmhouse. It was a pleasant little place, with dark green shutters and a climbing rose creeping over the door, though the plant was brown and sere now. I remembered vaguely once reading about how the front entrances of farmhouses were rarely used, but I could not bear to go searching for the back door, and, in any case, we did not know the family well. I grasped the iron knocker and let it fall three times before waiting a few minutes and repeating the action. I prayed someone would be at home; the thought of the long walk back to Grimly made me want to weep with exhaustion.

I was just about to give up in despair when I heard what sounded like a person coming downstairs. I knocked again, and caught the sound of grumbling from the other side of the door.

"All right, all right, no need to take on so!" The door opened to reveal a young man, probably in his mid-twenties, dressed in nightclothes and holding a candle. Behind him was the familiar rotund figure of Elsie Drabble. Upon catching sight of me, her jaw dropped, then she saw Sophie and looked even more startled. She threw the door wide open, ignoring the young man's confusion.

"Come in, come in, child! Heaven's sake, what brings you here at this time of night, and in your night things too! You must be freezing; come and warm yourselves by the fire!"

She ushered us in and down a short hallway to the big farm kitchen, where a fire was burning low in the grate. The young man blew on the coals and threw on some more wood, while Elsie bustled round lighting lamps and setting a pot of milk to warm. Sophie and I could only stand there, dazed, until she draped blankets across our shoulders and bade us sit down before we fell down. We gladly obeyed, collapsing onto the benches that stood alongside the scrubbed wooden table. I slipped the sack with its precious contents down between my feet. Sophie snuggled close and I put my arm around her.

"There we are," Elsie said, pushing mugs of warm milk sweetened with honey into our hands. "That'll warm you up. I never did see the like of it!" She was evidently bursting with curiosity, but restrained herself admirably while we drank. The fire was crackling merrily by now, and outside the windows the first pale fingers of dawn were beginning to lighten the sky, though the sun would not be up properly for some time yet.

"I'm sorry to wake you," I said, not really knowing how to start. Sophie was almost asleep, and I could feel myself becoming delirious with exhaustion. Elsie must have seen it in my face.

"Now then, none of that," she said. "You've clearly had a long journey; explanations can wait till morning. You'd best be getting to bed. The little one is about to nod off."

"I beg your pardon," I said, ashamed of my rudeness. "I meant to introduce you. This is Sophie Greythorne. Sophie, say how do you do to Mrs. Drabble." But Sophie could barely lift her head. Elsie was right; what we needed most now was rest.

"You can have the bed in my Katie's old room, and don't worry about rising early tomorrow – or should I say today?" she said. "You can sleep as long as you need." She led us upstairs into a small but well-appointed room with a large soft-looking bed. We washed our faces, hands and feet in water she'd had warming over the coals for the morning, and Elsie looked out clean night-things for us, for our own were stiff with salt and spattered with mud from the road. We tucked Sophie in, and the little girl was immediately sound asleep. Unexpectedly, Elsie drew me into an embrace.

"Sleep well, love," she said. "I don't know what made you flee the Manor, but I told you when we first met that you'd always be welcome here, and I still mean it. And you've no need to fear I'll tell anyone you're here, should they come looking."

"Thank you," I whispered, trying not to cry, for her kindness moved me deeply. I realized how much I had missed simple, generous human contact during my time at Greythorne Manor. Even growing up without a family, I had experienced enough affection at Brookvale that its absence had dragged at my spirits. Elsie left me a candle and retired herself, and, having stashed the sack – which Elsie had seemingly not noticed – under the bed, I clambered in beside Sophie. Only after checking she was fast asleep did I allow the full horror of the night to hit me. I rolled over and wept into my pillow until exhaustion overcame me and I fell into a deep sleep.

*

I slept without dreaming, and upon waking could not remember where I was. It was only as the fog of slumber lifted that the previous night's events came trickling back. It all seemed like a nightmare, and yet here we were. Sophie was still snoring softly beside me, but although I was weary and aching deep in my bones from last night's flight, I could not return to sleep. Instead I sat up, stretched and swung my legs out of bed, realizing I was also rather hungry.

Elsie must have been in earlier, for there were two gowns draped over a chair in the corner of the room. I discovered underthings tucked discreetly beneath them too, and two pairs of slippers lined up on the floor under the chair. One ensemble was child-sized, while the other looked like it ought to fit me. The girl's dress was rather old-fashioned, but the adult gown, though simply cut, was not unmodish. I assumed both had belonged to Elsie's daughters. I dressed, taking care to be as quiet as possible, and decided to leave Sophie sleeping. I told myself there was no need for her to be up, and that the poor child was quite worn out, but in truth I was not sure I could face her, knowing now what she was. Last night instinct had driven me to protect her and save us both; now, in the cold light of day, I knew not what to think. I tiptoed downstairs, shutting the door behind me, wondering how late it was.

I was quite surprised and not a little embarrassed to find it was going on for lunchtime, which explained my hunger. I found Elsie in the kitchen, which was filled with the hearty smell of baking bread. My stomach growled appreciatively and she laughed.

"I trust you slept well, then? Eh, you looked that worn out, I was quite worried about you." I assured her I had indeed slept well, and thanked her again for her hospitality.

"Nay, 'tis my pleasure. Anyone round here would do the same. Now, why don't we get some food into you?" She set a bowl of steaming porridge in front of me, and cut several slices of new-baked bread, which she slathered with butter and honey. I dug in gratefully, and for some minutes silence reigned, though I could feel Elsie's curiosity burning as if it were a tangible force. I knew I owed her an explanation.

Until now there had been no sign of anyone else in the house – for the young man I had met on our arrival was nowhere to be seen – but as I finished and pushed my bowl away a young woman came into the kitchen. She was pretty and fresh-faced, a few years older than me, and clearly with child – six or seven months gone, I guessed. When I looked properly and saw her flaxen hair and striking dark eyes, I reeled in shock, feeling suddenly faint, clutching the edge of the table for support.

"Why, my dear, are you all right?" Elsie asked in alarm. I nodded, though I was feeling far from well. Memories were flashing across my vision: a face in a portrait by a piano, and that terrible figure I'd found in the laboratory the previous night. How could she be there in front of me, as alive as I was?

"Oh, Mama," the young woman said, "is it not clear? She thinks I'm Lucy."

"Of course!" Elsie said. "Why did I not think of it? Nell, this is Isabella, Lucy Greythorne's sister. She's married to Michael, my youngest, whom you met last night. Great sakes, you must have thought you'd seen a ghost."

I smiled shakily, glad there was such a simple explanation, for after last night the appearance of an apparition would not have surprised me.

"I know we look alike," Isabella said with a smile, lowering herself to a seat opposite me. "Even though there was six years between us in age, people regularly mistook us for twins."

"Sophie is still sleeping," I said, realizing with a jolt that this discovery meant Sophie had *family* – an aunt, and soon a cousin too. "But I'm sure she'll be very pleased to see you."

Isabella smiled. "She won't remember me," she said, "for I haven't seen her since shortly after she was born. Lucy didn't come back to Grimly very often, and it was impossible for us to see her without Nathaniel's consent, although we tried."

"She wanted to," I said, thinking of all I had learned about the ill-fated mistress of Greythorne Manor. "She missed you terribly."

"How can you know that?"

And so I launched into my long explanation, starting with my arrival at Greythorne Manor and ending with the horrors of the previous night. And yet, I confess, I did not tell them the whole truth. I could not bear to reveal what Sophie really was; my stomach still lurched with revulsion every time I thought about it. Instead, I gave them the story I had first assumed to be true – that the Professor had been using Sophie to attempt to reanimate Lucy. Although a dreadful idea in itself, it was nothing compared to what had actually happened. When I described the desecration of her sister's corpse I noticed tears glinting in Isabella's eyes.

"The monster!" she spat, and I could not help but agree.

"And so," I concluded, "we fled here, for I couldn't think of anywhere else to go."

"You rowed right across the bay, in all that wind? You got through those awful rocks?"

I nodded. "Jonas brought us," I said, "and we were very lucky. I don't know what's become of the house or the Professor; I only saw it burning."

"And where is Jonas now?" Elsie asked.

I swallowed hard. "He didn't want to come with us. He's gone somewhere else, somewhere safe." I hoped he was at peace.

Elsie shook her head. "Well, as I told you when first we met, there have been terrible rumors about the Manor for years, and some frightful things said to be going on there, but this is quite unbelievable!" I looked at her closely; it seemed to me she spoke the truth, and that she did not quite believe my story. In the cold light of day the tale – even my sanitized version of it – seemed absurd even to me. And yet the truth was that much worse.

We were all sitting in silence, thinking over the strange facts of the case, when Sophie entered. She had managed to dress herself in the gown laid out for her, and appeared to have benefited from her long sleep. She had even brushed her hair, though it hung loose about her shoulders. Upon seeing Isabella she stopped, her eyes wide as saucers, and I hastened to introduce her.

"You look just like Mama," she murmured.

Isabella smiled. "I do, don't I? Would you like something to eat?"

Sophie nodded, then sat and ate quietly, and I made a mental note to ensure she took her medicine later.

None of us really knew what to say. Elsie and Isabella seemed to be contemplating my revelations, while I was wondering what was to become of me and Sophie, particularly if they would not believe us.

"Would you like to help me collect eggs from the chickens?" Isabella asked Sophie as she finished her meal. The little girl brightened at once. "And Miss Nell too?"

"You go ahead, sweetheart," I said. "If you bring us back lots of eggs we might even be able to cook one for your dinner."

Sophie bounced up and headed out the kitchen door, swinging the basket Isabella handed her. I rose more sedately – for my muscles were stiff and sore from the previous night's rowing – and helped Elsie clear the table, then followed Isabella into the large kitchen garden. Sophie was running around chasing one of the farm dogs, her hair streaming out behind her. She was clearly having a wonderful time, and I smiled as I watched her.

"You love her very much, don't you?" Isabella said, coming up beside me. "Almost as a mother loves her own child."

I nodded, realizing it was true; but if I loved her so, why did I now feel so revolted every time I looked at her? The child by rights should have been dead, and yet here she was, running in the wind like a normal eight-year-old. She was a triumph of science, and an abomination against nature. My conflicting feelings pressed at my chest in a way that was physically painful.

"It was very brave, what you did," Isabella said. I looked at her in some astonishment, for this sounded almost as if she had faith in my story.

"So … you believe me? I don't think Elsie does."

Isabella nodded. "I do. I knew my sister better than anyone, and the few times I saw her I could tell she was unhappy, although she was never explicit. Your story explains things she insinuated – I can see the connections clearly now, although I couldn't at the time. I only wish I hadn't been so blind, but such is the benefit of hindsight."

I felt my knees go weak with relief. "Thank you," I murmured, unable to fully express my gratitude.

Isabella gave me a shrewd look. "But you haven't told us everything, have you?" I felt my cheeks grow hot. "You strike me as an honest young woman, Nell," she continued, "and lying doesn't become you. It's written all over your face."

I hung my head in shame. "You're right," I said, "and I'm sorry. I just didn't know where to begin."

"The beginning is usually the best place, in my experience."

And so I told my story over, this time omitting and changing nothing. When I was done, Isabella stood silent for a long time, glancing from me to

Sophie and back again. I wondered if her feelings mirrored my own.

"He will come for her," I said, for I was never surer of anything in my life. "If he is alive, he will hunt her down."

"And you too?"

I shrugged. "He doesn't need me as much – anyone will do. But Sophie is his flesh and blood. He will not let her go." I did not need to add the real reason the Professor would seek her out. She was not just his flesh and blood; she was his greatest achievement. Without her, he was nothing.

Isabella stared into the distance, deep in thought. "Then we must protect her," she said at last. Her face was steely, and I imagined her sister making the same resolution before the headlong flight that led to her death. "She can't stay here, much as I would like her to; I can't conceal her, and I don't think anyone else ought to know what she is. You'll need to go far away, somewhere he would never look. We'll help you." She linked her arm through mine in a sisterly sort of way and together we strolled around the garden while Sophie ran and played in the weak winter sunlight. I was unsure what I felt, but it seemed that the child's fate was now indelibly tied to mine.

That evening at dinner we were joined by Isabella's husband, Michael, who had been out working on the farm all day. Sophie had eaten earlier, having an egg as promised; I had given her her medicine and put her to bed, then returned downstairs. Just as we were sitting down at the table there was the sound of a cart in the yard.

"That'll be my Jack," Elsie said. "He went off to market before dawn today – the middle of last night, really – so he'll be right worn out. Happen he might have some news, though." I knew she was thinking of Greythorne Manor.

Jack was a tall, ruddy-faced man with a bushy brown moustache and a ready smile. He seemed unperturbed to find a stranger in his kitchen; it was clear he took most things in his stride.

"Well now," he said, taking his place at the head of the table, "here's a to-do. What do you think's happened?" I wasn't sure if he wanted an answer, so I concentrated on my food. He glanced around the table, clearly enjoying keeping us in suspense.

"Greythorne Manor has all but burned to the ground, that's what!" he said, triumphant in his news. Elsie gasped as if she'd had no prior warning, or perhaps she was genuinely surprised to find I'd been telling the truth.

"Heaven's sakes!" she exclaimed.

"Aye. The village is in uproar. Fire's mostly out now, but they say last night it were blazing like a torch. There's hardly anything left of the inside – it's just a great stone shell. The constable went over this morning but couldn't find any survivors. Old Jakes said there was no sign of anyone, living or dead. They're saying that if those poor souls was stuck there, as it seems, they've been burned beyond all recognition and you wouldn't know them if they was sitting in front of you." He winked at me, and I smiled at his macabre humor, glad that he understood and that he would not turn us in.

I was overwhelmed with relief, then wondered what sort of wicked girl that made me. One day, perhaps, I would find it in my heart to mourn the Professor, but for now my ordeal was still too recent, and I rejoiced in the knowledge that he was dead.

Jack took a bite of food and chewed it slowly. No one else said anything.

"Gossip says the Professor was up to all sorts of ghastly things in that laboratory of his," he continued with some relish. "And did you know he was expelled from the university before he came here? He kept that pretty quiet, didn't he? Not quite the charming man we all knew, eh?" Isabella was looking down at her plate; I knew she was thinking of her sister. I caught her eye and gave her a sympathetic smile, which she returned.

"Come now," Elsie said, "you know them folks in the village'll make up the most ridiculous stories. It's a mercy it's all done and over, if there was wickedness, and of course we're all praying for the repose of that dear little motherless girl's soul, are we not?" It seemed Elsie, whatever her feelings about my story, understood at least that Sophie's and my survival was not to become common knowledge. "This is fine tea-table talk. How went the market?"

I had little interest in the rest of the conversation, so I just focused on my dinner and mumbled polite answers now and again if required. My mind was racing. If Jack was right, Sophie and I were now free – but what did that mean? Could we stay in Grimly? No: even if we could, I was not sure I wanted to. There were too many horrible memories just across the bay. But perhaps Sophie would be better off there with Elsie and Isabella and her family; she could truly have a second chance at life with those who loved her. I could go where I would, and in time she would forget all about me – a thought that made me want to cry. But then there was the complication of her medicine, and her true nature; Isabella had told me she would not be able to manage it, with children of her own to raise, and in truth I knew I was probably the best person for the task. But could I spend my days caring for a child who was not like other children, and who went against all the laws of God and nature? A child who, should she live long enough, might turn out to be just like her father – for was he not a monster too? I shuddered at the thought.

After the meal was over I made my excuses and retired to my room, but I was not tired. I sat in the window-seat and stared out at the moonlit farmland, Sophie's regular breathing the only sound.

I was miles away, lost in my thoughts, when there was a soft knock at the door. I opened it and found Isabella there, dressed in her nightclothes with a shawl round her shoulders. "I wanted to talk to you," she said. "May I come in?"

"Of course." I ushered her to an armchair before the fire and brought the chair from the dressing table for myself. We spoke softly so as not to waken Sophie.

"Do you believe he's dead?" Isabella asked without preamble.

"I don't know; I hope so. Is that wrong of me?"

Isabella shrugged. "Should he live he will always be a danger to you. I've been thinking about what you told me this morning. As I said, I would like nothing more for you and Sophie to stay here with us, but my heart tells me Grimly is not safe for you, and, well, I'm not sure how well Elsie would take to knowing the truth about Sophie. The child has suffered enough, and I think that for her sake you must go far away."

I nodded; I had reached a similar conclusion myself, though it pained me. "She may not live long," I said. "I have enough medicine for six months; after that, I don't know." I could feel my lip trembling. Isabella gripped my hand.

"Then love her," she said simply. "I know her very existence frightens and disgusts you, as it does me if I think about it too deeply. But first and foremost she is a child, my niece, and if she's not long for this world then I ask you only to love her as Lucy would have."

I could feel hot tears beginning to trickle down my cheeks, but I nodded, for I knew she was right.

*

Somehow Isabella squared things away with Elsie and Jack, but telling Sophie we had to leave a place where she was actually happy was one of the hardest tasks of my life. The next morning I broke the news to her about her father's death; she simply gazed at me with those dark eyes that made her seem old beyond her years, and said, "So he can't hurt us any more?" I felt my heart crack like porcelain, far more painfully than if she'd wept for him.

Elsie had arranged for us to go further north to a small village where her brother lived.

"I'll write to Charles before you go," she said. "He'll help you find work and a place to live. It's a shame you can't stay in Grimly, but I suppose it's for the best."

I wondered what Isabella had said to her, and whether the family would remember to keep our visit secret. I regretted the sadness we might be causing the

Greenslades, and my friends at Brookvale, with our subterfuge, but our supposed deaths really were the only way we could be safe both from the Professor and any authorities curious about the rights of a lowly governess to take permanent custody of an orphaned charge. I did not know if the Professor's former colleagues harbored suspicions about his research, or if anyone had ever tried to unravel the mystery of Alexander Grantham's death but, if they did, I did not want us connected with any of it. I knew that if the authorities ever found out the truth about Sophie, they would probably take her away and subject her to experiments and tests like an animal, and I could not allow that to happen. A new start would mean giving up the child's claim to whatever was left of the Professor's estate, but it was far better to start again in penury and safety than live comfortably but in fear.

A week after our flight from the Manor, we boarded the train at little Grimly station for our journey north. Elsie had generously donated us clothes and other small necessities, but we had little apart from what we wore and what I carried in our single carpetbag. Privately I mourned the loss of my books, but I hoped I would be able to replace them with time.

Boarding the train, I was taken vividly back to that first journey to Grimly that had started it all. What would have resulted had I heeded Elsie's and the

Greenslades' warnings all those months ago? It was a moot point regarding my own life, but even in spite of everything that had happened I had few regrets. It was certain that Sophie would still be languishing on that ghastly island, the unwitting subject of her father's grisly experiments; now, at least, she had a future, though I knew not what it might hold, nor how long it might last. As the train pulled away from Grimly I did not look back.

Epilogue

It has been nearly half a year now since that journey, and Sophie and I have managed to scratch a life for ourselves in the small northern village we now call home. We arrived late at night, exhausted and low in spirits, and were met by Elsie's brother Charles, who turned out to be very like her in his hospitality. We stayed with Charles and his wife Edith for several weeks, until we found a little cottage to rent. It is in a rather isolated spot, about a mile beyond the village, but it is comfortable enough, and I am glad to have our own place. Charles and Edith were very kind, but I worried constantly that somehow they would discover the truth about Sophie, although it was easy enough to pretend that she was simply a sickly child. I have taken a job as a teacher at the small local school, which Sophie also attends. It does not pay much, but enough to keep us in food and lodging. Sophie calls me 'Aunt Nell,' for we decided even before we left Grimly that the simplest explanation would be that she is an orphan and I am her maiden aunt, which is not so very far from the truth. I have all but given up dreams of a husband and family of my own, but, in any case, such prospects were never terribly realistic for me. Sophie is my family now, and that is enough. I still have occasional pangs of horror when I look at her, but then I remember Isabella's injunction to simply love her, and I am able to put them from me. In a few short years she will be a young woman, and I know she will be one of education and refinement. Like me, she will have to work to make her own way in the world, but unlike me she has beauty and charm, and is admired by all who know her. I am immensely proud of her, and I think Lucy would be too.

Our days are plain and unvaried, but they are calm and free from terror, for which I am forever grateful. We tend to keep mostly to ourselves, for I feel very protective of Sophie after our experience, and I am still learning whom I can trust here. But I also have another, deeper cause for concern; we are already three-quarters of the way through Jonas's supply of medicine. Although Sophie's day-to-day condition has improved markedly since being free of the Professor's constant, invasive tests, I fear what will happen should she ever not have access to the medicine.

I did not properly unpack the sack until we had been in our cottage some weeks; but when I did I discovered a torn, stained piece of paper covered with scrawling writing. It was a recipe, and I knew what it was for, but I could not bring myself to examine it too deeply. Conscious of our dilemma, however, I have taken it upon myself to learn as much about the science of reanimation as possible, for I refuse to believe there is not some alternative solution. I hope it might prove an advantage that the young curate, Mr. James, is himself an amateur scientist, and has quite an extensive library, though of course nothing dealing with the dark arts that so possessed the Professor. He arrived in the village shortly before we did, and despite my better judgment we have struck up an acquaintance. He is a kind man, only a few years my senior, and deeply interested in the world and its workings. We have spent many happy hours before his fire discussing science and theology, but I have not yet told him the truth about Sophie or the events that brought us here.

It has also been possible to obtain, by writing to certain city booksellers, tomes that *do* illuminate the practices of my erstwhile employer. These studies have proved extremely informative, for although the science remains highly speculative, the literature, I have found, has been quite practical in its advice. Behind our cottage is a small disused barn, and in the privacy it affords I have been undertaking some basic experiments. I have not been seeking to emulate the Professor's nefarious habits, of course, for they are abhorrent. I have been searching simply for a solution to help Sophie, and trying not to think about whether that makes me a hypocrite.

*

I look at Sophie now, seated across from me at the table, embroidering a shawl – the silk was donated by an elderly lady of the parish who has taken quite a shine to my dearest one, and indeed Sophie's exquisite work is worthy of the gift. She is, we have discovered, far more talented in this art than I ever was; the Brookvale mistresses would be proud of her. She looks up upon hearing a knock at the door. It is already dark outside, and it is unusual for callers to come to our isolated little cottage at that time of day, but on occasion the farmer across the way, Mr. Giles, has been known to bring us new bread if his wife has been baking, so we are not particularly startled. We live simply, without servants, and all help is welcome.

"See who that is, will you, Sophie?" I say, unwilling to look up from my writing. Of late I have been keeping a journal, if for no other reason than that reflecting on how far we've come helps stave off moments of despair. She rises obediently, laying her embroidery neatly on the table. I hear her walking out into the hall, a click and a creak as she opens the door, and then a single horrified cry: "Papa!"

I throw down my pen, splattering ink across the tabletop, and rise so fast I overturn my chair. I dash into the hallway, where Sophie is shrieking. She is wrestling with the door, trying to slam it shut, but a hand has snaked through the gap and grips her wrist. She stares at me, her eyes wide with panic. In desperation I batter with my fist at the hand clutching her. One of my blows hits home and the hand is withdrawn with a cry of pain, but before we can apply our combined weight to the door it is flung open in our faces.

I scream, because I cannot help myself. The face on the other side of the door is not that of the handsome, charming Professor; it is a monstrosity. The left side of his face has been melted away like candle-wax, and is now nothing but a mess of shiny pink and white scar tissue. The left eye droops; his brow is wrinkled and his scalp all but free of hair. It is only the color of his eyes – those ice-blue eyes filled with madness – that confirms his identity. My chest tightens and I can hardly breathe.

"Don't you like my face?" he asks, taking a step toward us. His voice is gravelly and menacing, roughened by smoke. "You should – you gave it to me. You turned me into a monster."

"No," I say, with an unexpected surge of courage, "you were a monster long before you met me." I block the doorway with my body, pushing Sophie behind me.

"Stand aside!" he orders. "I've come to claim what's mine!"

"There is nothing here for you." My hands are shaking and I clench them into fists. Perhaps it is the rising of some sort of maternal instinct, but I am prepared to die before I would let him take Sophie. Any ambiguity I have felt about her vanishes in the face of this threat. I had not known love could be so strong.

"She is mine," he says, his voice flat and laden with threat. "She is proof that I am the greatest scientist who ever lived." There is mania in his eyes that makes me shiver.

"No! She is a child, not your plaything. I will not allow it!"

He turns on me then, a knife gleaming in his hand. Instinctively I duck, shielding my face, squeezing my eyes closed. I am certain once more that I am going to die.

But the blow does not come. My eyes fly open at a cry behind me and the sound of metal impacting flesh. The Professor falls to the ground, his head hitting the stone step with a sickening thud. I turn around in amazement to see Sophie standing triumphant, the fire shovel in her hand. I know not how a little girl could find so much strength, but one edge of the shovel is wet with the Professor's blood.

I can feel tears running down my cheeks as I bend over the prostrate man. There is no pulse, and he is not breathing. I touch the scars on his face and am transported vividly back to that night in Greythorne Manor. How could one mere man be capable of so much evil? How could he see his own daughter as nothing more than an experiment? If that is all she is, then she is abhorrent, unnatural, an offense against the true order of things – but the child standing trembling above me is none of that; she laughs and cries and loves as readily as anyone I know. She has a brilliant mind and a strong empathetic streak and, seeing her in the company of other children, I have discovered she cares passionately about justice for the poor and downtrodden. Looking at her as if for the first time, I realize there is nothing abhorrent about her character; in fact, quite the reverse. And yet what kind of life can she possibly have now, with her medicine all but gone? I almost wish the Professor had killed me when he had the chance, if it would have kept Sophie healthy for longer. But he said himself that using my essence would be an experiment – that he had proved only that essences from the corpse of a direct family member had maintained reanimation …

I think again of that ragged piece of paper, tucked away in the back of a locked drawer where Sophie will never find it. I think of Jonas, a man who committed wicked acts but was not inherently so himself, who pleaded for redemption and has doubtless been shown mercy. I am not the Professor, for I do not seek personal glory, and I am motivated by love, the very opposite of evil. That, surely, makes us different.

I turn from the broken body to Sophie, who is staring at me wide-eyed but tearless. For long minutes she has not spoken, but now she crouches down beside me, slipping her warm little hand into mine.

"Is he dead?" she whispers. She does not seem sad; rather she seems afraid I will answer in the negative. I wrap my arms around her, pulling her close. This child is not a monster, I think, and she does not deserve her fate. And in that moment I decide.

"Yes, darling," I say. "But the best parts of him will always live in you."

Acknowledgments

Despite the popular image of the solitary writer in the garret, books are not produced in isolation. A great many people helped make this novel happen.

In particular, I'd like to thank my beta readers: Catriona Bryce, Pamela Burton, Mary-Anne Georgey, Paula Hanasz, Mary Hawkins, Rebecca Hilder, Bill Huff-Johnston, Lesley Jeffrey, Dave Mayes, Maxine McArthur and Chris Millgate-Smith. Their feedback was invaluable and prompted changes that solved many of the novel's initial problems. Sarah Bachelard, Sally Bachelard, Andrew Grimm and Neil Millar also provided incredible support, and Pamela Horsely's portrait of Professor Greythorne really helped bring the character to life.

I'd also like to thank the team at Momentum Books – especially Joel Naoum, Haylee Nash, Ashley Thomson, Patrick Lenton and Michelle Cameron – for making the publication process so painless. Kate O'Donnell was also a joy to work with and her edits improved the final manuscript immeasurably.

The enthusiasm, empathy and encouragement from my friends and fellow artists at Poatina Arts in Tasmania and the Sydney Artists Retreat was instrumental in helping me recover from a period of creative drought and gave me confidence that I really could be a writer. Without that support I probably would not be a published author today, so thank you.

Lastly, and most importantly, I'd like to thank my family. My parents, Amanda and Graeme, have watched this dream unfold over many years, and my husband, Tristan, has ridden this rollercoaster with his customary unflappability. Living with a writer is no easy task, so thank you for putting up with the highs and lows, for being my sounding board and taking even the wackiest ideas seriously, for feeding and watering me when I was in the "zone", and for believing in me when I could no longer believe in myself. I love you.